THE LAND OF DREAMS

and other stories

Chris Goff

Thanks to my wife for her encouragement,
support and editing skills; also to those friends
who have read some of these stories and
encouraged me to create this book.
You know who you are.

Prelude ~ Christmas 1968

The red London bus pushed through the congested traffic, as the few days before Christmas day loomed. Through the window of the bus, which was running with condensation, I could see frantic, overcoated, scarf-wrapped shoppers, searching for elusive gifts. I was sitting alongside my aunt Betty on the crowded bus, as it crept and jolted towards the department store where we were heading. This was my first experience in the big city, and I recall feeling nervously excited as to what awaited me at the store. There had been talk among the grownups, before we left my aunt's home, of 'seeing Father Christmas!'.

I wasn't that bothered if the truth be known. It seemed then, as it does now, that it was all a bit silly, and a lot of effort. I had never been amongst so many people!

The bus conductor, with his shiny ticket machine which spewed seemingly random tickets, moved through the bus as if he were an acrobat; dodging and weaving, jumping on and off the (sometimes moving) bus before disappearing up the winding stairs to the upper deck.

He remains in my memory as one of the first black people I had ever seen.

Soon we were getting off the bus and heading into the store. There seemed to be even more people inside the store than on the grey wet streets outside; the smell of wet wool mixed with the sound of piped Christmas music overwhelmed my young senses. I stuck by my aunt; I remember being fearful of getting separated and lost in this huge, bustling place.

Then we found ourselves in a long queue. The strange thing is that I can't recall ever meeting Father Christmas, although I guess I must have done.

The most memorable part of this treat was the motorised 'train' that took you to Santa's grotto. I can remember that when you reached the head of the queue, you were encouraged to leave your guardians behind to take the mystical trip to see the big man. I was seated next to a guardian that had *not* been left behind. She was a very large black lady who seemed to spill over into my seat.

Now, this may well have been the second black person I had ever encountered, but it certainly wasn't the colour of her skin that I remember all these years later. It was the aroma! I had never in my young life smelled the aroma that emanated from this lady. It was only in my teens that all became clear.

Fast forward to another year, probably early 1980s. It was after a booze laden night with friends, that we all decided to be bold enough and visit a newly opened Indian restaurant. As soon as I walked in, I was transported back to that cramped, motorised train. The smell was nothing more than garlic. But the 1960s was early days for the English palate, and my family certainly did not indulge in 'that foreign muck'. So, after many years, the mystery was 'sol-ved' as Inspector Clouseau would say, although even he would have recognised that smell a lot quicker than I did!

I love garlic now.

My aunt Betty passed away in April 2020;
she was old but died with Covid-19. I dedicate
the memory of Christmas 1968 to her.

Contents

A Drop of Oil   1

Frank and Edna   11

The Blackbird and the Whistle   19

The Land of Dreams   27

The Velvet Caress   39

Norman   43

The Butterfly Kiss   51

Andy's Little Rocket Ship 1955   59

Harry and the Time Traveller   65

The Actress's Bargain   75

The Boil on the President's Bottom   83

The Hood   95

Chuck and the Super   109

The House   121

Tim and the Whiskery Aunt   131

The Richmonds   141

The Second-hand Bicycle   147

A Million Housewives   159

The Coffee Shop   171

A Drop of Oil

Shelley was fat. There was no getting away from that word. I mean, it's not very nice to call someone fat, but there it is. Large, obese, porky, chubby; all good descriptive words, if not somewhat impolite, but for the sake of this tale we shall say Shelley was fat. So, there it is, and there it was. Shelley was fat.

Shelley wasn't unusual in her largeness; in her neighbourhood, there was a glut of fried chicken and pizza joints that delivered straight to her door, and into her gluttonous mouth. These fat saturated meals were washed down with litres of sugar laden cola and completed with doughnuts filled with the custard she particularly craved.

Shelley used to visit with other women in the neighbourhood, but she had started to become tired and the lure of daytime TV kept her inside. Slowly but surely her brain power and self-confidence dwindled as the girth of her body increased. Jim, her husband of 20 years, was the opposite; lean, muscly and vain. He seemed to relish his fitness and agility against his wife's morbid obesity.

He worked out at the gym every morning and evening and wouldn't let an ounce of saturated fat pass his cruel lips. Cruel, because he never missed a chance to ridicule his onetime sweetheart with jibes and insults regarding her size and eating habits.

So, Shelley grew fatter and increasingly unhappy, while her husband grew leaner and considerably meaner.

Shelley hadn't always been large; at 17, when she and Jim had first met, she had been lithe and athletic. She had won beauty pageants in their hometown and had been crowned *'Miss Beautiful'* of Bakersville, CA two years in a row.

With her long blonde hair, and legs that went on for ever, she gave the middle-aged judges sleepless nights. She filled their thoughts with lust and longing, leaving them gazing at their pot bellies and receding hairlines with the reality of lost youth and unfulfilled opportunities.

Jim and Shelley married in their hometown and the first year was spent getting their tiny home together. Shelley knew Jim had a roving eye and it wasn't long before he couldn't even be bothered to hide his infidelities from her.

When Shelley challenged him, he laughed and told her she should be happy that she had such a popular husband, and that she should be glad he stuck around, what with her 'being fat 'n all'.

The truth was, back then, she wasn't fat at all, but being told by an unfaithful husband for weeks and months that she *was* fat, had led her to think that she might as well be. 'What difference would it make to my life?'

When the 'closing down' sign appeared at the gym where he was a member, Jim was distraught. It wasn't only the exercise from the many machines at the gym that he would miss, but the exercise that he got with the Lycra clad housewives and girlfriends he sweet talked into bed, more recently into the bed that he and Shelley had once shared.

When the gym finally closed, Jim began building one at home. He was terrified his Adonis-like body would fall into ruin. He was even more scared that he wouldn't be able to tempt the liposuctioned, pumped, toned and tanned women into his bed. For weeks he hauled machines, bars and weights up the stairs to create his new workout area.

The day arrived when it was completed and he began to crash, bang and thump as he toned his beautiful body. Shelley's TV viewing was being ruined by all the noise emanating from upstairs, but she dared not say anything for fear of reprisal. On one such of these days, a tirade of swearing and cursing erupted from above while Shelley was trying to watch her favourite show '*Life Hacks with Dr Michaels*'.

'Get me the oil can Shelley, this goddamn machine is stuck!', Jim shouted from above.

It wasn't unusual for Jim to make Shelley fetch things for him. They were usually trivial things and Shelley made the long trip up the stairs, dragging her large and tired bulk up to give him what he needed.

She handed him the can, and he grabbed it from her, making a comment about how a small drop of oil makes a big difference to the moving parts. She was sure he was being suggestive, but this got big ol' Shelley thinking.

As she came down the stairs, she pumped a drop of oil from the can on the wooden steps and went down to finish '*Life Hacks*'.

Jim made a terrible racket coming down the stairs. There was an initial 'Whoa!', but this was soon followed by a sickening crunch and satisfying thud at the bottom.

'Oh dear, honey', she said to him, her large bulk towering over his prostrate body, 'what a mess you seem to have gotten into!'

She helped him stand as he wailed and cried out in pain, one leg at a very unusual angle.

'Let's get you on the couch.'

And so, with Jim pleading and crying for her to call 911, she diligently ministered to his needs. She bathed his cut head and tended his wounds.

With copious doses of painkillers and alcohol, Shelley cracked his leg back into roughly the right position.

She made sure Jim had no contact with the outside world, and when his mobile phone bleeped and chirped with missed messages and calls from his lovers, she stamped on it and threw it in the trash.

And boy, did that feel sweet!

Of course, Jim bitched and whined, but she was used to that. The difference was that now she had control and whenever he complained too much, she just turned up the volume on daytime TV.

Over the following weeks, Jim became more dependent on her. She fed him, washed him and cleaned him up when he soiled himself.

'Such a baby, Jim!'

Jim was apoplectic with anger, but there was little he could do. His legs would not allow him to stand and, every time he tried, his head unaccountably span and whirled.

Jim tried to control his diet, but Shelley was one step ahead. He ate what she put in front of him or he starved. 'I don't want that', he would grizzle when she would put chicken and fries on the TV tray, 'it's got too much fat in it!'

But Shelley would reply, in a soothing tone, 'Don't be silly Jim! I doubt it's got more than a drop of oil in it', and she would walk away chuckling to herself.

Then Shelley would retreat into the kitchen and prepare her meal away from Jim's eyes.

Salad and boiled fish were now her favourite meal, as she began to see the pounds slip away and the cheekbones of her once lovely face beginning to return.

Jim noticed her figure returning too, and started to pay her compliments when he wasn't grizzling about his food and the pain he was in. As the pounds fell off, Shelley began to experiment with her clothes. She would casually walk past Jim wearing a revealing top or overly short skirt. Jim pleaded with her for some relief for his frustrated state, but Shelley just walked away, planning her next provocative outfit.

Jim's inactivity and unhealthy eating habits began to show. He became frustrated with sitting on the couch all day but started to plan his day around the shows on daytime TV. The only show they watched together was '*Life Hacks with Dr Michaels*'.

After her afternoon run and workout in the gym upstairs, Shelley would settle herself in a chair and munch on an apple, while the good doctor explained another 'hack' to enrich life.

One afternoon while out running, she met a man. He was tall and fit, and used to run the same circuit as Shelley.

'Are you married?', he asked her one day while they were sitting on the park bench sipping water from their bottles.

'Oh no', she replied, 'I live with my brother. He has a very unfortunate condition. He is mentally deranged, you see; he had an accident and now he can't tell the difference between reality and fiction. It's very difficult, but I look after him the best I can.'

Before too long the man came to Shelley's house. Shelley introduced him to Jim, saying, 'This is my boyfriend, Lance. Say hello, Jim'.

Jim spluttered and spat. He tried to rise from the couch, but he was so fat now that this was impossible.

Lance looked on with sympathy and compassion. 'How sad it is, Shelley', he said, 'poor Jim. But poor you.'

'Oh, no matter', said Shelley, 'he's quite comfortable. I'm sure deep down he wants me to be happy. Let's go to bed. I'll just give Jim his medicine. A spoonful of oil. It's amazing what a drop of oil can do!'

Frank and Edna

Frank always enjoyed the bus journey from the small provincial railway station to the camp. Every year he requested the same two seats on the train, the same two seats on the bus and the same chalet at Sun Valley holiday camp. It was so nice to be alone with Edna; it seemed that the rest of the year was spent just surviving. Every day, he rose at 5am and was at the factory gates at 6am ready for his shift.

Frank and Edna had always got on well, ever since the day at school when she had cried about losing her pet rabbit and Frank had been the only one to offer sympathy. He was bullied because of that of course, but it was worth it. Edna meant the world to him, and when they married at 19, everybody agreed that they were meant for each other.

Their kitchen was a place of joy! Edna cooked the most wonderful food, and although it was often basic, it was made with love and eaten with gratitude.

Once the dishes were cleared and the small kitchen table was pushed back to the wall, Frank would turn on the wireless and they would wait for the valves to warm.

Then magic began to weave its spell in that small mid terrace kitchen. As the orchestras and big bands played through the speakers, Edna and Frank fell into each other and danced until they collapsed, exhausted, in the living room.

Cocoa was drunk, and up they went to their cold bedroom, where they giggled like teenagers until sleep took them. Then, much too soon, the cruel alarm clock roused Frank for another shift at the factory.

Every year, in summertime, they locked their small terraced house and with cardboard suitcases, scantily filled with summer wear, walked into town to get the train to Bramlington-on Sea.

They ate cheese and pickle sandwiches on the train as they watched the grey smoky sky of the city magically change, or so it seemed to them, into blue. The gold and green of the fields rejuvenated their tired and fuddled heads.

Edna always put a treat into her bag to go along with the sandwiches, and it was their own little joke that Frank always feigned surprise when he was given a fruit tart or a piece of Battenberg cake, which was his absolute favourite.

This year was no different; Frank opened up his sandwich bag to find two individually wrapped chocolate digestives inside. 'Oh Edna! How I love you!'

He wasn't usually aware of others on the train, but this year seemed different. There were two girls sitting on the opposite seats and they giggled to each other when he said this, while surreptitiously looking over.

As the bus approached the camp gates a representative climbed on board, welcoming the holiday makers with a loud and cheery 'Hello campers!' as he made his way down the aisle, chatting to each guest individually. Frank knew this redcoat; his name was Errol and he was the only member of staff that Frank had taken a dislike to. Errol had made some advances towards Edna several years back, and uncharacteristically Frank had squared up to him, warning him away from his precious wife.

This year, as in the subsequent years since the incident, Errol had avoided Frank and Edna and, as he walked past, he imperceptibly nodded his recognition of the fact. 'Well, never mind', Frank thought, 'he won't bother us again!'

'Well, Edna old girl, here we are again! Isn't it grand to be back! And the sun is shining on us!'

Every day, Frank was the first to rise and get the days essentials together. They didn't need much; a rug to sit down on and a couple of magazines to read. Frank was happy just to sit in the sunshine, while others around him laughed and played, taking part in the camp's organised games and soaking each other in the outdoor pool.

Frank liked the sound of laughter, especially children's laughter. Frank and Edna had never been able to have children; it was a sadness to them both but, as the years went by and grey crept into their hair, they took pleasure in the nieces and nephews that visited their modest home. As the day began to draw to a close, and the sun had begun to lose its warmth, Frank collected the rugs and magazines and thought about the evening ahead.

The evening had always been the highlight of the day for Frank and Edna; they loved to dance on the huge dancefloor. Frank considered himself quite a mover, as he whirled Edna around and around to the live bands playing swing and jive. Tonight was no exception.

Oh, how they danced! Frank hadn't felt so alive in years. The lights swung and flashed, illuminating the band, and the big mirror ball in the ceiling lit up the dancers as if they were in a Hollywood movie. This was the life!

Those not dancing were seated all around the edge of the floor at tables, drinking cocktails and smoking. It seemed to Frank such a joyful place. Frank felt that he and Edna were the stars of the show; it wouldn't be the first time they had won the 'dancers of the evening' prize.

But there was Errol, all Brylcreemed up in his evening jacket. Frank saw him talking to another Redcoat, pointing at Frank and laughing. After that Frank began to notice, for the first time, others laughing at him. Frank released Edna and made excuses to leave. Perhaps he was overreacting. Nothing a good night's sleep wouldn't cure.

Another year over. Frank got their meagre belongings together in the suitcases and, making sure that he didn't crush Edna's dancing frock, handed the luggage to the coach driver to be stowed. Just before the coach left the camp, one of the Redcoats came on board and handed Frank a large brown envelope.

'Open this later', she said, smiling affectionately at him.

'See you next year then?'; Frank smiled back at her.

'Yes, of course, wouldn't miss it for the world!'

Frank took the key from the string around his neck and slid it into the front door. He put the cases down in the hallway saying, 'Well we're home now love, shall I make us some tea?'

Frank made the drinks and, lowering his weary body into his armchair, he said to Edna, 'Not sure I'll be up to dancing tonight old girl, I'm a bit achy!'

Frank stared at his wife. It was a good thing he'd decided not to spread her ashes. He liked to see the urn by the fireplace every night when he returned home from the factory.

Frank put his tea on the side. 'I guess I made two cups again, Edna old girl. Silly me. I guess I thought you'd always be around.'

He opened the manilla envelope and pulled out a photograph. There was a note attached, which read:

'Dear Frank, we thought you would like this picture as a memento of your wonderful dancing this year! Love from the Redcoats x'

The picture showed Frank, a huge smile on his face, dancing with Edna. Although Edna, for some reason, was wearing a red coat…

'I guess I thought you'd always be around'.

The Blackbird and the Whistle

Not so long ago, a boy lived with his elderly mother in a small cottage deep in the woodland. The boy, Jack, loved the woodland more than anything else in the world. Well, that is, apart from his mother and his precious tin whistle. The whistle had been given to him by his father on his 12th birthday, just before his father had died in the harsh winter that year.

'This whistle was my Father's and his Father's before him', his father had told him on the evening of his birthday.

'They both learnt to play merry tunes and sad laments on it', he said. 'You will find that the notes play sweet and clear if you play from your heart. A tune played without any spirit is a dead tune, and it will die in the wind. If you listen carefully, you can still hear your ancestors play. When the crops are brought in, and when the winter wind drives folks inside their homes to sit by crackling fires and drink good ale, the whistle can be heard. My father told me that it was crafted by an old woodsman who spoke to the creatures of the forest and understood their ways.'

Jack's father made him a leather pouch, sewn with the cord of his grandfather's leather jerkin, and made a belt from the same leather so Jack could wear it when he went walking in the woodland.

Jack practised, and soon he made good clear notes that he wove together into tunes that caressed the woodland and soared away into the wind.

One fine summer's day, whilst Jack sat under his favourite tree playing, he heard a Blackbird singing close by. Jack listened carefully to the song, and then played a soft counter melody over the top; very soon, they both made the sweetest music that man has ever heard.

Jack returned to the tree every day and, every day, Jack and the Blackbird, who was very shy, made music together until the other creatures of the woodland sat quietly close by, listening to the wonderful sound.

On one such of these days, however, the Blackbird's song became shrill and jarring. Jack wondered what could be wrong until he looked up and saw a great Buzzard swooping low, trying to steal the Blackbird and his wife.

'No!', Jack shouted to the Buzzard, 'leave them alone!'

'Why should I leave them alone?', said the Buzzard in a high shrill tone, 'I have to eat as well! I can't grub for worms and insects like they do. I need fresh meat!'

So, the Buzzard swooped and thrust his powerful talons to where the Blackbird was, trying to get his meal. Jack shouted at the Buzzard, 'I will feed you meat, just leave them alone!'

'Yooou will feed me meat!', cackled the Buzzard, 'Well, you'll need to feed me every day then, or soon the Blackbird will be mine!'

So, Jack pulled open his lunch, which was wrapped in his handkerchief, and threw it to the ground; the Buzzard swooped and grabbed it with yellowed talons and flew off into the blue heights.

Every day after this, Jack returned to the tree, fed the waiting Buzzard and, when the buzzard had left, played his whistle with the Blackbird. Although Jack was hungry, every day his heart was filled with the music that they made together.

One autumn day, just as the air was beginning to chill, Jack returned home to find his dear mother had died. That evening, Jack cried and cried until the tears would not flow any more. He took out his old whistle and played the saddest, sweetest lament to his dead mother, tears rolling down the length of the whistle as he did so. Jack never noticed that the Blackbird, now with grey in his feathers, was sitting on the windowsill listening, and quietly accompanying his faithful companion in his time of sorrow.

When Jack returned to the woodland the next day he was bewildered. He could not hear the sweet Blackbird song anywhere! The old greedy Buzzard sat waiting for his meal as usual.

'What have you done, Buzzard!', Jack cried. 'Where is Mr. Blackbird?'

'I have not eaten him, Jack. He has flown away. You see, that's what birds do when they are very old.'

'Well, you'd better find your own food from now on then, Buzzard!', Jack said and then, with a *whoosh!* of wings, the old Buzzard lifted off the ground and disappeared.

Jack went home to his cold, lonely cottage and made up his mind that he would go to the big town, three days' walk away. Jack walked and walked and, as he walked, he became very sad. He had lost both his dear mother and his friend, the Blackbird, in just two days. He was very hungry and very tired. Soon the town came into view. Jack had never seen the town before and thought this might be the place he could become happy again.

Now, Jack was unaware of the ways of the townsfolk here, but it was a very bad place and, before he had been there very long, he was set upon by a gang of villains. They pushed him to the ground and one of them took Jack's shiny whistle from its pouch and blew into it, making shrill and discordant notes. They kicked and punched him and looked through his pockets for money but found none. Then they stamped on his whistle, flattening it on the ground.

'Leave him alone!'

They all froze. Standing in front of them was a lady. She was the most beautiful thing Jack had ever seen. She had long black curly hair which reached down to her waist and she wore a black and yellow dress which was sheer to her body.

'What do you want of him?', she said.

'We want his money!'

'Then take this and spend it in the tavern!', and with this, she threw a handful of silver coins at their feet. (She knew the tavern owner and would get him to slip something into their beer, so they had heads like toads for a week or more).

Jack picked up his broken whistle and, replacing it in his pouch, thanked the lady and began to walk off down the track, back into the woodland where he felt safe.

'Wait!', she cried out to him, and gracefully moving towards him, kissed him on the lips and pushed a parcel into his hands. 'You will need this for your journey, Jack.'

Then turning swiftly, she slowly walked back along the track. As she walked, she whistled a tune; oh, how it reminded Jack of his Blackbird's song!

As Jack walked, with the tune playing inside his head, he unwrapped the parcel to find a note inside.

It read:

'This has been waiting for you, made with the songs of birds.'

In the parcel was a whistle, made of fine silver, and as he put it to his lips to play, the sounds of the woodland burst in joyful song from the trees.

And Jack joined them, with his new silver whistle, and a new song in his heart.

The Land of Dreams

It's funny how certain things stay with you years after the event. For example, Mrs. Markham's seaside bed and breakfast dining room.

Taste.

I have never tasted milk as sweet as the milk at Mrs. Markham's breakfast table. I couldn't wait to rise in the morning and place that cool glass to my lips. As an adult, I hunted the sterile supermarkets for another taste of childhood, but it was not to be. I know now that it was probably some specific breed of cow, roaming leisurely, chomping on grass and breathing clear air, that has long since gone.

Smell.

Mrs. Barker's perfume from the adjoining table, musky and sensuous, although I didn't know those words back when I was 10. It was years later, walking through a department store, that I smelt Mrs. Barker again. Of course, it was not her. I followed the poor woman all over the store, just a few steps behind, wallowing in the memories and taking lungfuls of the heady scent as if I were going to suffocate.

God knows what I would have said if challenged. But the senses are powerful things, as this tale will unveil.

The B&B had 6 rooms; these were all occupied in the summer months when we took our annual holiday. Every year new faces and every year new children to be avoided. My parents would try to engineer friendships that would ease the burden on them to have to entertain me; it never worked out, unfortunately for them.

Every year the same two faces sitting at the adjoining dining table; Mr. and Mrs. Barker. Conversations between my parents and the Barkers became commonplace, as recognition over the years led to a less formal relationship.

Mr. Barker was a seasonal overseer at the local amusement park 'The Land of Dreams'. Oh, how I loved that place! Over the years, as my parents got to know the Barkers, three tickets used to appear on our table at evening mealtime. Mr. Barker, who was at the park all day until late evening, would charge Mrs. Markham to surprise us with the tickets for the park, along with our evening meal.

Mrs. Barker, who took her evening meals at the B&B, showed great delight in feigning surprise and shock at her husband's generosity and cunning.

It's worth accounting the effect Mrs. Barker had at evening mealtimes on the male population. As Mr. Barker was absent, Mrs. Barker became the focal point of the room. The married men, sitting with their families, would gaze in sorrowful longing at this creature of beauty, whilst their sunburnt wives looked upon her with loathing and envy.

She had an easy style and her long red hair would often be tousled and tangled, adding to her natural allure. The other women would glare at her and then subconsciously touch their own hair, stiff and perfect under layers of cheap lacquer.

Mr. Barker was somewhat older than his wife and quite old fashioned, even for the early 1960s. He was rarely seen without a white shirt and black tie, and highly polished brogues. I remember staring at them as much as I stared at his young wife's nyloned legs, emerging from her mini skirt.

I'm sure the other men, my father included, wondered why Mrs. Barker had married an 'old stuffed shirt like Barker!'. But my memories of him were of a generous and witty character, totally absorbed and in love with his wonderful wife.

They had no children of their own, so when our family became friendly with them, he used to seek me out and make me laugh with his exaggerated Brummie accent, and stories about how he lost part of his middle finger. The stories changed with every telling, but I believed every one of them.

The Land of Dreams was an old park. Built in 1880, it still retained the old-fashioned allure and quaintness that led hundreds of visitors through its huge iron railed gates in the summertime, as it had since its opening years ago. I can't recall many details of the park, only that it had an atmosphere that modern parks don't have. There was a home-made feel about it. Advertisements for the rides were hand painted, and most of the rides built by craftsmen and joiners who put their own stamp on them, much like the masons who left their mark on old churches and cathedrals years ago.

Grotesque and comical gargoyles dripped water onto the heads of modern worshippers hundreds of years later, although the devilish gargoyles took a different form in the park. The odours altered as you walked through the park. Candyfloss, toffee popcorn, onions, diesel and chips, all mingled with the smells that the patrons brought with them: cheap perfumes and aftershaves, beer and hastily washed sun-lotioned bodies.

The wooden floor of the 'Halls of Wonder!' had the smell of beeswax and bubble-gum, a smell that if I concentrate enough these days I can still bring back to my senses. The two attractions that are very clear in my memory all these years later are the huge wooden rollercoaster and the aforementioned 'Halls of Wonder!'. I visited the park several times over the years and loved every minute of it. I only ever rode the coaster once. It was fun and thrilling, but my pleasure in it was watching others as they screamed and laughed when the cars dropped down the huge wooden chasms, making that slow clacking sound on the way up, and then speeding up on the descents; CLACK! CLACK! CLACK! CLACK! as the open car careered down.

There used to be a real live brakeman; white vested, acned and greasy, hanging onto the side of the car to slow its pace as it picked up speed. The youth always performed his acrobatics for the most attractive occupants.

The 'Hall of Wonders!' was just that. I'm sure if it were still around today, I would be underwhelmed; that's how memories work I guess, but back then it was a magical experience. Inside the building were a hall of mirrors, finger smeared and wonderful, and penny arcades, real old big chunky pennies with Queen Victoria glaring as you pushed her into the silver slot. A walk-through 'Alice's Wonderland', an indoor carousel and then onwards to the 'House of Wax'. This was my favourite. There were several themes inside, including celebrities, most of whom are long gone now, both in real life and in their original wax form, melted for candles maybe. Then on to the best part, a gruesome torture chamber. I can remember one poor soul lying on his back for years, while a swinging blade moved ever nearer to his stomach, threatening to spill his guts all over the plastic rat-infested floor. Every year, much to my childish disappointment, his guts were still intact as he glared, terrified, skywards.

Mr. Barker was very proud of this exhibit, and he never lost his enthusiasm when talking about it to the many who passed through its doors. 'A piece of history!' he would proudly announce, to anyone who cared to listen.

It was the last time that we were to stay at Mrs. Markham's. I guess the seaside town had grown too familiar in our eyes; it was as if there was nothing new to excite us as a family. We had explored the area many times, visited all the tea shops, ice cream parlours and the local library. Even our favourite ice cream parlour had the same 45s in the jukebox as it had done the year before. It was as if the town itself was tired of trying. We were done.

But this wasn't the real reason we never returned. The real reason was that Mrs. Barker disappeared.

It was the last evening of our holiday and my father had been moody all day. On the short, but steep, walk down to the beach, he had twisted his ankle and he complained and whined for the rest of the day. 'Oh, Will, don't make our last day miserable! Come on, let's get an ice cream; one of the special ones you like. Think of Davey, he goes back to school on Monday!'

My father didn't think of me though; he rarely did, and he wasn't in the frame of mind to be placated with an ice cream. He continued to lay on the sand with his ridiculous red sunhat resting over his face.

Even the Barkers had been different at breakfast. I sensed some friction between them, which I had never noticed before. Mr. Barker's brogues were still polished, but I noticed his shirt was grubby around the neckline. Mrs. Barker was unusually reserved, and kept her eyes averted from our table.

My mother and I visited The Land of Dreams together that evening. Father remained at the boarding house, moody and quick tempered. It was the best evening ever. I came away with a furry spider, with a rubber bulb attached to a pipe, which actually moved along the floor as you pumped the bulb.

The next morning, the Barkers' table was vacant; the dining room was full of whispers and quick glances. Someone asked Mrs. Markham if she had a radio, and she brought back a huge transistor, tuned to the BBC. I still remember the formal BBC voice from the loudspeaker years later.

'A man has been arrested and charged with the murder of his wife in Thanet. He was an employee at the amusement park, The Land of Dreams; he will be formally charged later this week.'

It was a few weeks after we got back home that I found a newspaper on the kitchen table.

'Man convicted of murder. Albert Barker has been tried and found guilty of the murder of his wife, Doris Barker, nee Smith, at the pleasure park known as The Land of Dreams, Thanet.

'Mr. Barker stated in his address to the court that on the evening he killed his wife, he saw her in sexual congress with another man in a maintenance shed where he had gone to collect some oil for one of his attractions. Mr. Barker chased the man, to no avail, but on his return took his wife to the attraction known as 'The House of Wax', where he bludgeoned her to death and left her amongst the grisly exhibits. He surrendered to the police on their arrival at his lodgings in town.

'He will be hung by the neck until dead this coming Thursday.'

I placed the paper back on the table and went to my room. On my bedside was the spider from that last evening. I picked it up and thought about the holiday and the car journey home. I remember having my first bout of hay fever. Father was getting irritated at my constant sniffing and, reaching into his pocket, pulled out a handkerchief. Even through my mucus blocked nose, I could smell the musky perfume that has stayed with my senses all these years.

The Velvet Caress

I was a seducer. Always was.

My tanned and voluptuous body was made for caressing. Curves that ached for sensitive hands to embrace them. A waist that these days would be called 'hourglass'; unfashionable perhaps, but it got me attention. Sometimes the wrong kind.

My long stately neck was ornamented with semi-precious stones, completed with a head that was decorated with silver on both sides.

I sat in the window and looked out at the people passing on the sidewalk, as I had been doing for many days. Perhaps today would be the day when I met the right person. He would have to be sensitive. The last one was a brute and I still bore the scars of his temper meted out on me.

Maybe it was time for another makeover. I had them periodically. Sometimes the full works; body buffing and a spray to bring back my lacklustre colour. Mostly I just had some minor cosmetics to cover up the aging process and hide the scars from poor relationships.

I couldn't count the times when I had sat alone in the corner of a room, bolt upright, watching others enjoy themselves. I was conceived for attention and praise, but these days rarely got it.

I recalled the last party I had been at; some dolt spilt a full glass of whisky over me. Laughing, he just got up for a refill. The whisky felt like acid as it dried and congealed on me. If only Bob had noticed, he may have offered to assist. But Bob was busy charming the socks off another young thing, while I remained glued to the floor, unnoticed, in a roomful of wannabe musicians.

I wasn't surprised when Bob left me. Commitment wasn't his forte. A new model had taken his eye, all pert and glamourous. Loud and flashy. He couldn't even break up with style. Had to knock me about a bit first.

I sit in the rocking chair at the window and await the inevitable surreptitious glance from the sidewalk by a potential suitor. And then the bargaining will begin. It's becoming mundane now, but the process is age old.

Look. Assess. Commit.

Today is my lucky day. A young man walks in, all curly hair and boots.

'What can I do for you, son?', my owner says.

'I'd like to look at that guitar in the window', he says. 'She's a beauty!'

And then I'm off. Sensuously encased in velvet and carried to the waiting car.

Not bad for 100 years old, even though I do say it myself.

Norman

Norman was a very shy and lonely man. That was until he met and fell in love with an opera singer.

Their courtship was brief and exciting; Norman had never even experienced companionship, let alone wild and passionate lovemaking. She moved into his small flat with grand ideas of 'upgrading'. She was bright and funny, wore outrageous clothes even when she was off stage, and drank like there would be no gin for a year. In fact, she was everything Norman was not. And he was devoted to her.

In his quiet times Norman wondered what she saw in him, but he pushed these thoughts away as he became scared of where they would lead. He continued to make love to her while Mozart played loudly on the record player. His now wife writhed and accompanied with gusto.

Months and years passed; Norman continued to be puzzled as to why this vibrant woman found him attractive, but he had a new-found confidence and, after work every day, visited a local bar to drink and chat with the regulars.

He wondered whether he should have an affair, but he had very little energy for this. He then returned home to Mozart and everything that went with it.

One day when Norman returned home, two tickets for a trip abroad sat on the kitchen table. Norman had never been further than Bognor, so he was nervous about this new development.

'It will be wonderful!', his wife exclaimed as he stood with the tickets in his hand. 'The South Sea Islands! Beaches and sunshine!'

Norman wasn't so sure and became anxious. He had a fear of the water, specifically paddling. He had discovered this on holiday in Bognor as a boy. His mind had become fixated on what was under the water in the mud and sand. His overbearing father called him a 'wimp' and the rest of the holiday was spent in the dingy caravan reading about superheroes.

Holiday attire was purchased. Norman's consisted of some new vests and a racy pair of red swimming trunks bought by his wife from an upmarket fashion house. It appeared to Norman that his wife was enjoying the clothes shopping as much as she would enjoy the actual holiday.

Norman began to worry about where all the money was coming from and realised one day before the trip that he did not love his wife anymore. He wondered if in fact he had ever loved her at all. Perhaps the passionate lovemaking and Italian singing had clouded his mind?

The gin had begun to affect his wife's career. She forgot her lines on stage and no amount of cleavage could cover this up. She lost work but sang even more loudly at home, much to the annoyance of the neighbours who, not being Italian nor interested in opera, shouted English insults through the walls.

Norman started to become unhappy again, but this time he couldn't be alone with his unhappiness, as Mozart's long-playing masterpieces were a constant companion, accompanied by a redundant opera singer.

But they went to the South Sea Islands.

Norman found that he liked the bikini clad girls and the cocktails but hated the muscle-bound men who would dive into the sea at every opportunity to recover a conch shell or spear a fish. Of course, his wife loved it all.

She spent most of her time on the beach looking at these muscle-bound men, trying to catch their eyes before they dived into the sea for another show of machismo.

They hired a small motorboat to visit a neighbouring island. Norman disliked the chugging boat and he disliked even more his wife's singing as the small craft pushed its way through the sea. The wind stole his wife's straw hat and it blew away over the water. She wanted Norman to chase after it as 'it cost a great deal', which made Norman even more resentful about the trip. The island was theirs for the day. They saw no others, and, after lunch which was supplied by the hotel, they explored it. There were caves and caverns, and lots of palm trees. Norman wondered about wild animals and snakes but kept these thoughts to himself.

They sat on a rock overlooking the sea, Norman wearing the red trunks which he had reluctantly put on before the excursion.

'Dip your feet in the water Norman, it's lovely!'

Norman ignored the request. The last thing he wanted today was to be stung or attacked by a foreign sea creature.

'Go on Norman! Oh, you are a wimp!'

Suddenly Norman was back in Bognor with his brutish father.

'Bloody wimp you are lad, get in the water like the other boys, or go back to the caravan and stay there!'

Norman turned to look at his wife. It seemed to him he hadn't looked at her properly for weeks, maybe months. The once smooth skin had become bloated and veiny from excess alcohol and overeating. Her ample bosom had started the inevitable journey south, and her makeup, once so perfect, had become slapdash and clownlike.

Gingerly, Norman put his feet into the water. It was actually quite nice, cooling and somehow adventurous. 'More, more!', his garrulous wife bleated at him, 'stand up, stand up, let's see you paddle!'

Norman, emboldened by his initial effort, lowered himself into the water. No sooner had his feet touched the bottom, than he felt a sharp object cut into his foot. 'Ow!', he cried.

Norman's wife erupted in merriment. 'Wimp, wimp, wimp!', she chanted.

Norman reached down into the water and, feeling the object of his pain, pulled a large conch shell from the water.

'It's a shell Norman, just a shell, what a baby you are!'

Norman looked at the dripping shell in his hands and, without much thought or remorse, brought the shell down with a resounding and satisfying crack on his wife's head. Norman's wife fell back on the rock and sang no more.

It took Norman a good while to get the boat to the cove and load his substantial wife onto it. By the time he made it back to the mainland, he had the story about the tragic accident sorted and managed to conjure up enough distress to convince the police of the genuineness of it.

Norman took the now claret stained swimming trunks off in the hotel room, washed and dressed himself before having one last cocktail in the hotel bar. He was overjoyed, although he dared not show this, to receive all his drinks 'on the house'.

The funeral passed without much ado. One of Norman's cousins pulled him to her breast for solace. He quite enjoyed that.

There were some of his wife's old thespian colleagues at the ceremony and, much to Norman's irritation, they insisted on performing his wife's favourite arias. But he thanked them and showed the right amount of sorrowful gravity as they recalled tedious stories of opera life.

Norman's life went back to how it was before. Norman was once again a very shy and lonely man.

That was, until he met and fell in love with a figure skater…

The Butterfly Kiss

Frank thought it would seem reasonable that being lost in the woods should have made him slightly anxious. The fact that he was lost in a forest made things even worse. The fact that the forest was in Amazonia just put the icing on the cake.

'I mean', Frank said to himself, 'hey, I've been lost before, right?'

Yes, Frank had been lost before; he almost made a habit out of it. If there were certificates or diplomas for getting utterly and hopelessly into a predicament, Frank would be having graduations on a regular basis.

Frank thought that it was very unsportsmanlike of his so-called friends to have left him alone in camp while they went off for a jolly with the local tribe. He wasn't really interested in trying out hallucinogenic frog spawn or drinking alcoholic beverages mixed with saliva from old hags. He wasn't interested in whatever the locals did to get off their shaved and pierced heads.

Camp was a miserable affair, with mildewed tents and mud everywhere. Frank spent the first couple of hours tidying his kit, or what was left of it. The adventure to the Amazon had seemed a good wheeze when they were all drinking in the London pubs. All the plans, maps and gear, not to mention guidebooks, were gathered together in Frank's flat in anticipation of the big departure day.

Frank looked around the camp and realised that most of the gear had either rotted in the damp humid jungle or been stolen by inquisitive locals. The guidebooks had lasted about a week before they fell apart. They were next to useless anyhow.

There were a few hours of daylight left before the celestial switch was turned off and the jungle was plunged into utter darkness. The sun here was either too hot or not there at all. Frank thought it was totally unfair. In fact, Frank thought thc whole trip was completely unreasonable and very uncomfortable. He wished he were back at home in his small but comfortable flat.

Now he was bored.

His so-called friends were probably going to stumble back in the early hours rambling incoherently about the deep spiritual visions they'd had whilst licking frogs. He couldn't bear that. Frank decided he would go for a short walk; not a long walk as he was self-aware enough to know that his sense of direction was poor. Aside from that, he walked very slowly as he was terrified that a snake would jump out on him and inject its deadly venom. He wouldn't like that either.

Frank liked walking on his own as it gave him time to think. This adventure had been fun initially; they were all in high spirits, glad to leave the suffocation of London and the ties that held them down. They were all bachelors and had oppressive jobs in grey poky offices, returning to grey dingy flats after a day's ledgering and filing.

The bond between them began when they all read the same book. The book had caused a stir amongst adventurous types, a supposedly true tale of the search for a city of gold deep in the Amazon jungle. The images that the book cast wove spells around all of them until, one night in the back bar of an old pub, one of them had exclaimed, 'Let's go there!'.

The noise and gaiety from the adjoining bar seemed to dim for a second as they all looked at each other, considering each other's reaction to this announcement.

A day or so into the jungle, cracks had begun to appear between them, and they quickly realised they were woefully underprepared and out of their depth. But still they persisted. They were never going to find a city of gold, but some real Indians would be wonderful! So, they walked deeper into the jungle. They became lean and hungry. Insects had left festering sores on them, and their feet had become swollen and painful. After three weeks they had finally come across a small native tribe who seemed friendly enough. So, they made camp and agreed that they would spend their final night there before returning home.

As Frank walked through the forest and thought about going home, he became aware that he hadn't been paying attention to his surroundings. Frank hoped he wasn't lost again, but he knew he was, and that was just the icing on the cake. Frank sat down, resting his back against a huge tree. He was tired and very hungry. He kept his eyes peeled for snakes and jaguars.

Out of the corner of his eye, he saw a blue flash. And then there it was, the most beautiful butterfly he had ever seen. It was the size of a saucer; its wings were azure blue, edged in white. It flew around him; Frank could feel the soft movement of air as the large wings fluttered past his face. Then the butterfly landed on Frank's arm; it remained perfectly still, allowing Frank to study it.

Frank had never really thought much of wildlife; most of it scared him. He often wondered why he had been swept along into coming here. As a child he had been stung by a wasp and since that day he had avoided anything that flew or slithered. As Frank watched the butterfly, he saw that it was not beautiful after all.

Its thorax was covered in thick brown hair. To Frank's horror, but also fascination, it had a long curly tongue which resembled a liquorice whirl.

The tongue unfurled and began to lick his arm. Then with a flutter of its wings, the butterfly rose into the air leaving an incandescent blue blur in Frank's eyes.

How long Frank sat under the tree he could not recollect. Years later when recalling the tale, he wondered why he hadn't tried to make more of an effort to get back to camp, but a strange feeling had enveloped him after the butterfly had left.

Night had fallen, but not in Frank's eyes! He was seeing the surrounding forest in bright surreal colours. Trees were communicating with each other with bright flashes of cobalt; they flashed constantly between each other. Frank was mesmerised. As he stared into the forest a strange, yet clear, vision began to unfold before his eyes.

Structures began to form; they began to take shape as temples and grand habitations. In Frank's world morning had broken but, in reality, it was still the dead of night. The buildings now encircled Frank.

And they were gold, a deep yellow, rich gold. The city of gold!

And that was it. Frank sat with his back against the tree, for how long he couldn't remember, watching the comings and goings of the ancient peoples of the fabled city.

Then, when the vision began to fade, he stood and followed a luminescent glow back to the camp.

It was morning then. Wearily his friends rose and, after a meagre breakfast, began to boast about tales of drunkenness and hallucinogenic visions. They said that Frank had missed out on an important part of the trip. Frank remained quiet and nodded, agreeing that he had been a fool not to accompany them.

Years later, Frank returned to the Amazon. He tried to find the spot where he had the vision but alas, it wasn't to be. The forest that Frank and his friends had walked in had been razed to the ground by the logging companies. It was on his return to London that he got into a conversation with a lepidopterist. The old man had collected butterflies in the Amazon for many years.

There was one, however, he had never been able to collect. It was a large specimen with bright blue wings. It was said by the Indians to have great powers if it landed on you. It was believed that it would lead you to great wealth and the holy city of gold....

Andy's Little Rocket Ship 1955

Andy loved space. He loved it so much that he pestered his father for weeks on end until eventually, worn down with the disappointment that was etched on Andy's face, his father bought him a telescope.

The rectangular box had an illustration of huge gaily coloured planets and bright white stars, just like the ones in the comic books he read. And what a fine telescope it was! All polished brass and gleaming glass. Andy set the telescope up next to his bed and pointed it up through his window to the heavens. If only night would come!

And, as is the way of the world and its slow but regular movement, night did arrive, and Andy slept only briefly as his concentration that first evening was out into the vastness of space.

Andy spent every night gazing into the night sky. He never grew weary of the countless patterns of the far galaxies and bright celestial bodies that filled the eyepiece of his telescope.

He especially loved the moon.

The craters and mountains became so familiar to him that they almost felt like home, as he visited them night after night. But although Andy was glued to his telescope, and the wonders he saw through it, there was something missing that he couldn't identify.

And then, one night, it became clear what it was that he was missing. He wanted to go into space and walk on the moon!

So, Andy began to build his own rocket ship. Painstakingly he copied, from the cover of 'Space Cadet!', the design of the ship.

Nuts, bolts, tape, paint and glue. Silver foil to help protect its blast through the atmosphere. Anything Andy could persuade his father to spare from his shed was used to build the craft. His bedroom was filled with plans and parts for his rocket ship.

Finally, the day arrived, and the craft was complete. Fresh silver paint covered the skin of the craft, and some of the carpet as well!

Packed into the shiny new cockpit was Andy's beloved telescope.

That evening, as night began to fall, Andy rose from his bed, dressed himself in his old clothes (the ones he used to wear when he played in the garden) and began preparations for lift off.

Once the checks had been completed the countdown began.

5…4…3…2…1…

Lift off!

Andy braced himself. At first, nothing happened. Then, as he began to worry that he had missed something vital from the ship, it slowly, but powerfully, lifted itself from the bedroom floor and………whoosh! …out through the bedroom window into the night air.

Andy was flying! The ship pushed itself up through the chilly night air leaving his small hometown below. He could just about make out his house and see the light that shone from the open window. Higher and higher he flew, the ground and his hometown now barely recognisable as just a few dots of light in the darkness. He was now through the clouds and heading for outer space!

As he broke through the earth's atmosphere, the silver foil working a treat, the window of Andy's cabin was filled with the bright glowing moon.

The spaceship flew faster now as it pushed and pushed towards the moon. Andy prepared himself for touchdown. This was going to be tricky, but he had seen Capt. Storm do this many times in '*Space Cadet!*' comics.

And then he was down. He'd landed on the moon! A cloud of dust rose around the craft as it settled down. Andy climbed from the cockpit and put his feet on the moon's surface. He looked across the lunar horizon and saw the bright blue and green sphere of earth. His home. Far, far away.

Reaching into the spaceship, he pulled the telescope box out and looked at it. The picture of the moon that he had gazed at so many times in his bedroom paled into insignificance with the real thing.

He slid the scope out and pointed it towards the earth. Slowly, turning the focus, it came sharply into view.

Andy moved the telescope until he could see his country. And then delicately moved it until he could see his hometown. Yes! There it was, there! As dawn began to break, he was sure he could see his house. There it was! His bedroom, with the window still open from where he had flown out last night.

There was his bed; both his mother and father were there. But there was someone else in the room.

The doctor stood over Andy's body after he had examined him. Andy's mother was sitting in a chair sobbing, his father standing upright at the door. The floor to Andy's bedroom was littered with cut up cardboard and tins of paint.

'I'm sorry, Mrs. Allen', the doctor said, 'the cancer must have moved quicker than we thought. It appears that Andy slipped away last night in his sleep.'

The doctor closed Andy's eyes and stroked his pale lifeless brow. 'I am so sorry.'

Of course, if the doctor had examined Andy thoroughly from head to toe, he would have seen a coating of strange grey dust on his feet…

Harry and the Time Traveller

Murder. Just a word. Four consonants and two vowels. Most of us will never commit a murder; sure, we may think about it at times. We may even make plans in our heads on how to commit the perfect murder. But we will never take the next step.

Harry Richardson was the exception. He had never once even thought about murder. If you were to ask anyone that knew Harry, they would say, 'Harry, commit murder, that's absurd! Harry…never!'

Harry was the grey man. Never once spoke out of turn or caused a ripple. His lawn perfectly manicured, his black Ford Popular immaculately polished on the drive. But on the day the man from the future arrived, Harry killed. Well, sort of…

Harry was middle aged and would be described by the populace as 'grey'. He made no waves in his life. He went to work in his navy suit and spent his leisure time dressed in a carefully selected range of beige.

Harry was a confirmed bachelor but was furiously in love with Shirley from the typing pool. Shirley was married to a brute of a man. But although Shirley moaned and grizzled about her life with Rex, on Monday mornings when the girls got together to discuss and gossip about their weekends, Shirley giggled like a schoolgirl. Harry could only watch through the office glass and wish that he could take Rex's place.

One Monday, the girls in the pool were huddled around Shirley, passing her tissues, and making more of a fuss of her than usual. As Harry walked past with the excuse of needing a piece of typing done, he saw to his horror what Rex had done. Shirley's face was bruised and swollen, and, from his brief glance, Harry saw a missing tooth.

Harry returned to his desk distraught. If he had been a different person, he might have taken the opportunity to actually talk to Shirley and offer her sympathy. Who knows where that might lead him! But this was not Harry's way. He did what he always did; he sat and furiously checked the paperwork on his desk.

The only glimpse of Harry's anger on that day was a curt reply to the tea lady when she asked him if he wanted, 'tea or coffee love?' When he sharply replied, 'Tea of course!' she wondered if Harry had piles and if he did, she understood his tetchiness.

Harry returned home for his supper, and the light programme. Slumped in his living room was a stranger. A burglar! But fast asleep! He should call the police. As he walked over to the phone, the man groaned and mumbled something.

Harry stopped dialling. The man was dressed in a strange manner. He wore running shoes and strange shiny trousers with stripes up the sides. On his top half he wore a sleeved vest emblazoned with the words 'The Beatles'.

The man groaned. 'Please put the phone down. I'm not here to hurt you; I shouldn't be here at all.'. As he rose from Harry's couch, he stumbled and quickly sat down again.

'I'm sorry', he said, 'the transfer this time was a little rough. I'll be fine soon, and I'll go. You'll see I haven't stolen anything.'

There was something compelling in this man's manner. Harry was intrigued; how did he even get in? Harry walked to the back door and found it, along with all the other possible entrances, secure.

'Do you study insects?', Harry asked the stranger.

'What…er, no…oh, I see the T-shirt! No, they were a rock band I loved.'

Harry's look of confusion prompted the stranger to continue. 'Look, you wouldn't comprehend if I told you. In a few years you may understand, but all you need to know is that there has been a mistake. I'll let the agency know there's been a balls-up, and I really am sorry I landed up in your front room. Once I get myself together, I'll be gone. Do you have a glass of water please?'

Harry moved towards the kitchen to get the man's water. What was he doing? Treating this interloper as a guest! He really should call the police. But Harry was curious.

At that moment, a strange noise broke through Harry's musing. The stranger began talking into a small rectangular device.

Harry placed the glass of water in front of the man and sat down opposite, looking at the strange sight. The stranger seemed to be talking to someone far away; perhaps the object was some kind of walkie talkie? Harry had used them in the war, but this one was much smaller. The stranger finished the conversation and got up to go.

'Look,' the man said, 'it really is against all protocol for me to have been found by you, but you mustn't tell anyone about me, OK? If you do, things will go very badly for you. Just pretend that you never saw me, and things will be fine. Look, I tell you what, I like you, looks like you have had a rough day. Anything I can do for you?'

Now this was the point when Harry should have said what Harry always said, 'No, I'm fine, just dandy, you go ahead, nice to have met you'. But it was true, Harry's day had been bad, and instead he replied, with a wry smile, 'Well, you could do Rex over for me!'

So that evening, for the first time in his life and as is often the way with feelings, Harry told a complete stranger not only about his love for Shirley, but about the hate-filled and vengeful thoughts he had about Rex.

'Look' said the stranger, 'I can't begin to tell you how much of a mistake it has been landing in your front room like I did, it never happened before. That thing you saw me speaking into, well it's knackered, and I need that for accuracy amongst other things. Time travelling is a rough gig at the best of times; I'm getting too old for it really, but it was the agency's mistake this time! Hey, that's a laugh isn't it, too old for time travel!'

Harry didn't really understand a lot of what the stranger told him, but time travelling! Now that was something.

The stranger (he wouldn't tell Harry his name) told Harry that he worked for an agency which specialised in manipulating the past to change the shape of future events. As the time passed, Harry became convinced that this man was who he said he was, a time traveller from the future. He was supposed to have 'landed' in a quiet cul-de-sac just around the corner, but the small device had 'cocked the co-ordinates up'. Harry hadn't heard the phrase 'cocked up' before, but he liked the sound it made, and he stored it away for future use.

It turned out that 'manipulation' was another word for assassination.

Harry thought. And Harry wondered.

And Harry said, 'Could you *kill* Rex?'

The stranger didn't even flinch.

'Sure, it would be easy. But what's in it for me?'

Harry thought. And Harry wondered.

'Nothing', he said. 'I have nothing, but I will keep quiet. Just kill Rex. It will be perfect; no one will suspect, and no one will have known you were here.'

'I like you Harry, and you have been kind; where can I find this Rex?'

'He goes fishing after work every Friday, drives down to Richmond. It's Friday tomorrow; you could do it then?'

'Consider it done, Harry old chap. Remember, we never had this meeting; it's all been a dream.'

Then much to Harry's alarm, but also delight, the stranger once more got out the small device, touched the screen a few times and disappeared from sight.

'Well I never!', thought Harry, 'what a turn up for the books! Guess Rex is screwed now!' And shortly after a light supper, he toddled off to bed.

Harry gazed at Shirley through the window of the typing pool on Friday; he felt invigorated and bold. She looked up at him from her typewriter and gave him a shy smile and a small wave; she was being coy about her missing tooth he supposed.

Harry walked back to his desk, a new spring in his step. 'Monday', he thought, 'I'll show sympathy and concern, then perhaps I'll ask her to go to the cinema!'

On Monday, Harry wore his new light blue suit to work, with freshly polished new brogues. He wanted to make a lasting impression on Shirley this morning, as he gave his condolences.

As he approached the typing pool, he could see all the girls huddled round as usual. But where was Shirley? Perhaps she was so distraught she had taken the day off? One of the girls spotted him and beckoned him in.

'Oh Harry', she wept, 'Shirley is dead! Someone cut the brake pipes on Rex's car which he lent her for the weekend. She was off to see her mother and had a fatal collision on the motorway!'

Harry felt sick. What had he done!

'Harry, Harry, are you OK? You've gone very pale?'

'Did you know that Shirley thought the world of you, Harry? She said she was going to finish with Rex after the weekend and thought you two might get together. Oh, I'm so sorry Harry!'

Harry collected his briefcase, got into his shiny car and drove home. When he got into his living room, he cried out, 'Where are you, where are you, you damn time traveller…come back, oh, come back!'

Harry waited and waited, and the clock's hands kept on turning, and no stranger turned up.

Time. It's a funny old thing.

The Actress's Bargain

In that very phony grand town called Hollywood, there lived a very beautiful actress.

Gracie Silveira played princesses and virginal queens during the day (her speciality) and in the night-time she played, with some gusto it must be said, the whore. She writhed and twisted in her black silk sheets with stars and starlets, male and female. Crew members, carpenters and set designers fell in love with her beauty on sight and she never spent a night alone.

Needless to say, she was very popular, and there wasn't an evening where she didn't attend one of the grand and debauched parties hosted by producers and the very wealthy that lived in that town.

Gracie had bright ginger curly hair, green eyes and an hourglass figure that met her outfits in all the right places. But very few things in the world are perfect. Unfortunately for Gracie, she had a voice that could cut cheese, break glass and send mice running to cats for safety.

This was of no consequence.

It was the early days of filmmaking and there was no technicolour to show the red hair or green eyes, and there was certainly no sound for the cinema goers to hear the screeching and piercing voice which would surely clear any theatre.

The piano scores that accompanied the movies in those days hid a multitude of splutters, stammers, whines and poorly rehearsed accents that, if there had been sound, would have left the audience perplexed and probably scarred.

Gracie's real name was Dolores O'Sullivan. The second she stepped off the ship from Ireland in New York harbour, she became Gracie; she thought this was a film star's name. It turned out she was right. Gracie was at the top of her game; producers and directors loved her looks and winning Irish smile, and the parts for princesses and virginal queens kept rolling in.

The audiences never seemed to grow tired of the often-repetitive stories, as long as her bosom heaved and her eyes fluttered. The dollars continued to grease the movie making wheels and Gracie continued to hear 'Action!' both day and night.

As is the way of things, progress thrills some but destroys others. Production lines were killing the craftsmen, and the new technology in cinematography was sending shivers down the spines of the actors who never had to learn lines or be aware of their elocution.

The moment that Gracie's first sound reel came out of post-production, the director and producer knew there was a problem. Her voice just didn't translate onto the silver screen. In fact, it was painful. Everyone scratched their heads. They didn't want to lose Gracie, but hell, the public wouldn't pay 35 cents to have headaches after a showing.

Gracie became fearful; she was used to being loved and adored, she was at the peak of her career and she was a prima donna. She could see starlets with voices that translated to silk on the screen making their way up the ranks, albeit via the casting couch.

Then, one evening at a party, she met Nick. Suave and sophisticated, she was impressed by his winning smile and easy charm. She had met many like him before of course, but there was something behind his sunglasses that warned her to be wary.

He was a lover like no other. There seemed no end to his enthusiasm for her. As they writhed in passion, she saw red flashes flicker in his eyes, and bestial grunts emanated from his mouth. Exhausted and sore at the breaking of dawn, she confided to him her fears for her future.

'I can make you the most famous talkie star ever', he whispered seductively in her ear.

She listened. He talked. But what he said made her shiver with fear.

'You will have a girl child from our union tonight', he said. 'When your time comes, you will look after her for five years. When those five years are up, I will return to collect her, and she will accompany me to the dark shores of Hell. In return, you will have the voice of an angel and will flourish in your career. If you renege on this deal, you will regret you were ever conceived.'

And then, without any further ado, he dressed, replaced his sunglasses and swept out of Gracie's bedroom, to return in 1,825 days.

The crew were amazed at the transformation in Gracie. She became a voice coach for the up and coming starlets and made herself invaluable to the tinsel town moguls. Her movies became more popular than ever; she had added a darker side to her character roles, which came as a surprise to her peers; 'I wonder how this all happened?', they mused.

Gracie's child was a joy. She grew up with the smell of greasepaint in her nostrils, and the love and companionship of the film crews around her. Everyone adored 'Little Grace' and she was spoiled rotten.

1,825 days had passed, and Gracie had never forgotten the pact she had entered into. As Nick walked into the room, she welcomed him as if she couldn't wait to give her child over.

'Oh, Nick!', she cried, 'how wonderful our daughter is! Before you take her, you must see her acting skills. She has learnt so much from being around the sets all her days…. listen.'

Nick grunted in irritation but cast his eyes over to his doomed daughter.

Gracie had voice coached Little Grace for many weeks especially for this day and Little Grace was ready for the short performance. She collected herself together and began to give a speech from Macbeth. Unfortunately for Nick, his daughter had inherited her mother's original voice. Gracie had tutored the girl to exaggerate this and project her speech loudly with all the squawking, shrieking and squealing that she could possibly muster.

The sound she made was horrendous.

It was a disastrous triumph!

Nick exclaimed, 'By Christ! She's worse than all the Banshees of Hell...keep her!' And with that, he departed for the dark shores of Hell. Alone.

The Boil on the President's Bottom

There once was a spoilt boy, who became the leader of a great country. But let's not get ahead of ourselves. Let's start from the beginning.

Harold was born into a very rich family and was told on a regular basis, 'You can do anything you want, honey!' and then he was lavished with kisses from his doting mother. She wasn't sure he could do anything, as actually he was pretty foolish but hey, a mother's love and all that.

The other kids often ridiculed him for 'being so dumb'. It was true, he was pretty dumb, but this didn't really matter as he was able, with the help of extreme wealth (in the form of pocket money handed to him on a silver platter), to buy into any gang he wanted to.

The gang may not have wanted him, as he was often very embarrassing, but the money that came from his deep silk lined pockets helped to grease the wheels.

Childhood turned into youth and, although never an attractive person, neither inside nor out, he became popular with attractive girls wanting to climb the ladder.

So, they climbed into his bed, much to the irritation of his lusty peers, and often repeated his mother's mantra, 'You can do anything you want, honey!' With that, after the ordeal, they may receive expensive trinkets or at least a gem of wisdom from his pouty lips.

Harold believed that he was not only very wealthy and popular, but that he had great wisdom; those that were in his company hung on his every word, nodding like the dogs in the rear parcel shelves of their automobiles.

As the years of youth turned into adulthood, Harold's empire grew. Unfortunately, his wisdom and humility didn't grow alongside the copious hotels and golf clubs that now littered the great land. Few dared to disagree with the great man; after all, their jobs and livelihood often relied on his cash.

Harold continued to hear the words he loved to hear so much, 'Yes. You are right'.

Harold was perplexed; he had amassed great wealth and he had a beautiful wife that hung on his every dollar. He even attended prayer meetings every now and again, as he thought it was probably best to keep the big man on board.

But there was something missing.

Harold had simple tastes. Well, it probably suited his character. Not for him the exploration of fine food and expensive restaurants. Harold enjoyed nothing more than a night in front of the TV watching his favourite news channel and eating hamburgers.

He knew about literature and music, but somehow he never quite 'got it'. He enjoyed the odd theatre visit, but this was mainly to check out the showgirl's legs.

When others spoke of the brilliance of Shakespeare, he would reply 'Yes, great guy, super guy, met him once, needs a haircut', and he left them speechless, but nonetheless nodding affirmation.

Now, for all of Harold's failings, the one thing you could say about him was he loved, and I mean LOVED, his country.

He flew a flag on every one of his buildings and was often heard praising the greatness of his kind who came to the land many years ago, to tame it and teach the savages about the great white man in the sky.

One morning, while looking in the mirror and teasing his hair into a new style, assisted by copious amount of hairspray ('the girls go crazy for my hair!'), it suddenly came to him what he was missing in his life.

He wanted to be President.

The television in the adjoining room was broadcasting a speech from the current one and it made no sense to him. This guy was always making a fuss of the poor and underprivileged; Harold thought it was about time the poor and underprivileged pulled their socks up and stopped whining. He would make his country greater than it had ever been! 'I can do anything I want!'

It was a grand inauguration. Harold had all the people around him that agreed with him; there was lots of backslapping and cheering as Harold climbed into the military helicopter to fly to his new presidential home. He couldn't help but smile, as the outgoing president leant over to shake his hand. What a sucker!

Now to make his land great again! The first thing he wanted to do was make sure that no more undesirable people came into his land. 'His land', that sounded so good on his lips!

So, he built a wall around his country. He didn't like or trust the people on the other side, and he wanted to keep them away. Apart from the ones that cleaned his presidential home. They were different. In Harold's mind this showed to others he was not prejudiced if he let the strange swarthy foreigners clean his house.

Harold had found his rightful place in life, or so it seemed to him. There were plenty of people that bought into his simplistic ideals, and those that didn't? Well, Harold simply fired them.

He found this was a most convenient method of running his great country. Harold was more than convinced that he had always been destined to be president. Perhaps those occasional prayer meetings had been worth it after all? The man in the sky was on his side.

Things seemed to be going well for Harold until one day at breakfast he noticed his bottom felt, well, uncomfortable. He reached into his presidential pyjama bottoms and had a feel around.

Hmm, definitely not quite right. There seemed to be some kind of lump on one of his presidential cheeks.

Now, the presidential bottom is not a thing that is easily addressed in matters of state, so Harold kept the situation close to his, well, bottom and continued making important decisions about the welfare of his country.

The problem was that he couldn't concentrate. Every time he was supposed to be focussing on what his advisors were saying, his thoughts crept back to his bottom, and the tingling irritation he felt on it.

The following morning things were no better. In fact, Harold had trouble sitting at all. He went to the bathroom and squatted over a mirror. His large bulk wobbled as he tried to see the problem, but it was too difficult and he toppled over, cursing as he fell.

That day in meetings he fired three members of his staff. One dared to suggest a relaxation of taxes on the very poor, and the other two, in Harold's eyes, seemed to agree with the first.

'Get away from my table!', he cried. He seemed to remember something about a table in the Bible, so he thought himself very clever. The three stunned staff members sheepishly left the room whilst Harold thought about the lump on his posterior.

It was no good. He couldn't stand it anymore. He had to confide in someone and get some help. He turned at first to his spiritual advisor.

The spiritual advisor told him that with enough faith the lump would go. And so, they put their hands together, closed their eyes and prayed. It was an awkward moment for the advisor. He didn't know how to pray about the president's bottom, but he made a fine effort.

'Dear Lord, please help our beloved President in his time of need. Please take away the lump on his, er,' (he was always told in theology school to be specific), 'posterior, so he can sit comfortably again and be healed of the pain in his,' (he stumbled a bit here), 'ar…bottom. Amen.' Short but to the point, he thought.

The following morning the lump had grown to the size of a small egg and was very painful. Harold cursed and swore, as he gingerly walked around the kitchen, and when morning worship came on the TV, he threw his coffee at it and shouted, 'You're fired!' as he waved his fist at the ceiling.

The presidential doctor was summoned. Harold lay face down on the bed while the nervous doctor examined the presidential swelling.

'I think it is nothing but a boil', he said, 'I will lance it and you will have relief!'

So, the doctor prepared the lance, and with some local anaesthesia gingerly pushed it into the fiery boil.

'How odd!', he thought.

Nothing came from within the large swelling. He tried again, this time pushing deeper into the president's corpulent cheek….

The president screamed. The president wailed, and jumped from the bed, cursing the incompetent surgeon.

'Get out, get out…you're fired!', he cried, and went back to his room to lay face down on his silken bed, soaking the pillow with un-statesmanlike tears.

What could he do? Then it came to him.

He rang his mother and explained the situation to her. 'Mommy, help me, I'm in so much pain!' He spared no detail of his unfortunate predicament.

'Oh, my poor baby', she cried down the phone. 'How awful you must feel!'

She gave him the details of a top surgeon and told Harold to see him at once as she couldn't bear to think of her baby in so much distress.

The surgeon lived far away, so Harold chartered his private jet and set off, supported by strategically placed cushions, to find relief.

The plane streaked through the sky and Harold was looking forward to landing, gently he hoped, and getting to see the top surgeon for some relief. Unfortunately, there was a great storm raging and the plane hit turbulence which bucked and rocked the aircraft. Harold would have liked to have fired his pilot, but even his stupid mind told him that this wasn't the best idea.

The plane began to lose altitude as it hit the eye of the storm and began to tumble from the sky. The very apologetic pilot informed the president that a soft landing was not on the cards, and in fact he should prepare for a crash landing! Harold awoke with a mouth full of sand, and a very bad headache. As he gingerly raised himself up and looked around at his surroundings, he could see the smoking wreckage of the aircraft, and the desert that was its final resting place.

What to do! He carefully stood and was pleased to find that although bruised and battered, he could walk. As he began to stumble along through the sand, he realised with some elation that the pain in his posterior had gone! The boil must have burst on impact with the ground.

What a mess he was in. His clothes were in tatters, his face covered in cuts, and his hair, well, even without his beloved mirror he could sense it was a mess.

He floundered on for a day and night through the desert until he saw lights! 'I'm saved!', he cried.

As he got closer to the lights, he saw that they were floodlights on top of a great wall. Barbed wire ran along the base of the wall, and there were spikes all along the top perimeter.

As he sat thinking what to do, he could hear the sound of traffic coming from the other side.

'Help! Help!', he cried, but no one heard him. The wall was too high and too impenetrable.

As he sat, helplessly looking at the lights and listening to the sounds of civilisation from the other side, he wondered to himself, 'What kind of fool would build such a wall!'

The Hood

The headmistress was a bit eccentric. No, let me rephrase that - barmy. I bumped into her one rainy afternoon in the quad, her hair looking like she had been in a recent altercation with a power socket. I made the usual glib comment about the weather. 'Oh', she said, 'there's no such thing as bad weather, just a poor choice of clothing.'

I always disliked the enforced small talk you were expected to make when bumping into someone you don't really respect that much, but social etiquette demands a response, however superficial.

I wanted to say, 'Well, quite, but you insist that we wear these bloody formal clothes so now look at me, soaking wet!' Of course, I didn't. I smiled, nodded and went on my way to find the small child I needed to assess for psychological trauma. No wonder these kids are traumatised, the bloody headmistress is as crazy as a loon.

She may have been crazy, but she was correct on this occasion; it was galling however that she told me something that had been my mantra for years.

Even as a youth I had been obsessed - is that too strong a word? - no, it's not; obsessed, with having decent clothes. I don't mean the clothes from the fleeting fashion parade, but the clothes of utility.

Duffle coats, work shirts, heavy wool jumpers, logging boots, assorted hats, all were stashed in my residential wardrobe, ready for whatever the English weather could throw at them. The headmistress would have been proud if she had known this; I may have even got a house point.

Before the story continues, it's worth mentioning that the wearing of these clothes did me no favours in day to day life, especially when younger. The English weather was for the best part clement, the bulkiness of thick wool and heavy boots were more of a hindrance than anything else. I longed for snowdrifts and torrential rain, but they rarely came. If there was a chance of a frost or heavy shower, I became excited and raided the wardrobe for suitable clothes. As you probably guessed, I overdid it every time.

I fondly remember the time I was shopping in town with my mother. I had a teenage birthday approaching, and from out of the corner of my eye I saw them!

A pair of pine coloured high laced boots, with a dark brown collar. I can still remember the advert which was on a stand behind them; a picture of a denim clad youthful couple, check shirted, boots on, heedlessly wading through a stream, evidently in the American wilderness. 'Totally waterproof, and warm down to minus 20°!' I had seen the first import of Timberlands.

That day I was bought my first, but not last, pair of Timberlands. Until they sold out to fashion. How absurd to wear something meant for rugged outdoor pursuits in a town! But of course, much to the chagrin of some friends, I did.

So, picture if you will a twenty-year-old male, cajoled into going to a nightclub in the late 1970s in the middle of summer. Not for him the flowing stonewashed jeans, open necked shirt with obligatory medallion, nonchalantly strolling into said club, cool evening breeze tousling long locks of blow-dried hair.

The word to pick up on here is 'breeze'. This refreshing draught of air for most would offer respite from the day's oppressiveness. For me, however, it meant the concern that more sinister atmospheric conditions might arrive.

Typically, I would arrive at the club in Timberland boots, logging shirt and duffle coat, with the possible addition of a wool sweater 'just in case'.

The reader will probably guess that the evening was awkward. A few years down the line and I would have been taken for a Village People fan, but for that moment in time, I was just hot. Extremely hot, and not, it must be stated, in a good way.

So, there I was, back in the day, primarily dressed for monsoons and snowstorms, but encountering no more than moderate breezes and light showers.

As I looked down at the playground tarmac, I could see the phosphorus lights of the school reflected in the puddles at my wintery wet feet. The globs of chewing gum that covered the ground looked like stars, the whole vision reminiscent of a Van Gough picture.

I was a confirmed dreamer, but the school timetable jolted me back to reality. It was Friday and the end of the day drew near, counted down by the sonorous clanging of the bell.

The weekend had arrived at last, a break from bells and the roar of children, and an escape to the wilderness. Although it was November, it was mild, and I was well prepared. A lightweight tent and well stocked rucksack were sitting in the hall ready to go, alongside my new purchase.

Of all the outdoor wear I had bought over the years, this one was the most satisfying. A green army surplus jacket. But not just any; there were thousands of them for sale out in the market. No, this was a genuine Alpha industry, pre-owned 1970s M65, field jacket. If there was a king of jackets, this one had the crown.

Dear reader, be patient for just a short while before we continue with the tale. I must describe the reason why this jacket, which actually makes the wearer look like a sack of potatoes (with the exception of DeNiro in Taxi Driver), is so great.

The material is a sanforized cotton, which makes it hard, if not impossible, to tear or snag. The pockets are HUGE, you could probably store tent and sleeping bag in them without the bother of a rucksack.

It has a heavy brass zip, none of your YKK rubbish and it has a feel about it that you could face any quest in it, and the jacket would protect you.

It had one fault; a concealed hood, pretty rubbish, thin flappy material rolled up in the collar of the jacket, but even this will come into its own later in this story.

The Peak District National Park signs began to appear, as I headed for the small village where I would leave the car to begin my trek into the wild. The clement weather remained and, after a couple of pints in the local, I wandered off to find my spot for the night. It was not difficult to find a secluded spot away from prying eyes in this part of the country, but I strode as much as I could into the terrain, just to be sure.

The spot I chose was in a small glade of woodland surrounded by the majestic peaks. The evening light was stolen by the night; as the last tent peg was hammered in, the only illumination was the brilliant moonglow casting eerie shapes over the surrounding peaks. An owl hooted, adding to the serenity of my home for the night.

The long drive and the real ale had its desired effect on me; I crawled into my sleeping bag. The air had turned chilly, so I pulled the beloved army jacket over me for added warmth.

And I slept.

CRACK!

It felt like I had only been asleep a short while; as I opened my eyes, I could tell that night hadn't ended yet, but some fool was firing a gun!

CRACK, CRACK, CRACK!

I felt anxious; this wasn't at all what I had expected. Groggily, I clambered out of my sleeping bag and, wrapping the jacket around me, I unzipped the porch of the tent and poked my head out. I must have been dreaming.

The quiet pitch had transformed itself into a muddy blasted wasteland. I could see this in snapshots as carbide lit the night sky.

'Bloody farmers', I thought, 'always shooting something.' But even my thoughts didn't ring true. This was more than some overzealous farmer, was more like…

The deer hunter.

Bud pulled the jacket around him as the rain lashed around the camp. There were no distractions; there was rain, gunfire and explosions, the soundtrack to his life these past few months in Dong Nai. Bud took a draw on his cigarette, shielding it from the driving rain. The gunfire drew nearer, his stomach spasmed, knowing that orders to move forward were minutes, if not seconds away. This place was brutal. Humanity had quickly dissolved after the unit had arrived in camp several months ago. Men who would have hesitantly yelled at a barking dog at home, now routinely put bullets through fellow human beings' heads.

Bud shouldered his rifle as the expected order was bellowed through the rain and commotion of the chaotic camp. Men began to check equipment and put on helmets and camouflage in readiness for the push forward. Bud had dreamt about Lucy last night. It wasn't an erotic dream; life had become too grim to even think about that. Sure, some of the men went off to use the local brothels, returning late at night with liquored heads and new lifeforms multiplying in their groins. These visits left Bud cold, and he remained in the bars drinking, or stayed in camp while his comrades looked for brief moments of engineered closeness.

The previous evening Bud had remained in camp. He had dreamt badly the night before. Dreams were rarely good in this place, but last night's dream was powerful and strangely real. He had seen enough death during his time here, had lost some good buddies and, as was to be expected in such a treacherous place, his own mortality had been at the forefront of his mind. But last night's dream.........

There was no sugar coating; Bud had seen himself die. Seen the small Viet Cong soldier rise from the jungle floor and, as if in slow motion, take sight on him and pull the trigger. Bud saw the shiny bullet hurtle through the rain; its point perfectly aligned with his head. Normally he would wake at this point, but this night was different. He felt the molten lead smash into his skull and the metal cylinder create a chaotic storm of bone and brain which exploded from his head. Still he saw; saw himself slump to the floor, while the Viet Cong moved over him to kill another of the U.S. Army.

So, as the boys snuck out of camp to find overpriced beer and willing women, Bud sat with pen in hand composing a letter to his Lucy and, when it was finished, he slid it into an envelope and then into a cellophane chips wrapper. He sealed it with tape, kissed the package and got himself ready for another sleep disturbed night.

The next day as the orders came to advance on the enemy, Bud felt strangely light and calm. As he pushed through the wet undergrowth, everything seemed oddly cinematic and familiar. When the Viet Cong soldier sprang from the jungle floor and levelled his rifle, Bud knew his reactions were too slow for return fire. The last thing he consciously thought was how wonderful the raindrops looked as they fell through the air, and how the small silver thing that exploded from the Viet Cong's rifle would finish the desolation he felt...

The shooting had quieted but the rain fell in torrents as I gingerly explored my campsite. It was still very dark, and my phone's light barely showed any of the surrounding area. For the first time since I had bought the jacket, I reached back to free the hood. As my cold fingers fumbled with the Velcro flap and found the hood's material, I pulled it and hastily covered my soaking hair. Everything seemed quiet now, and I wondered whether I had imagined the whole thing. Annoyed with myself for getting so uptight, I turned and carefully began to walk back to my tent.

On the ground in front of me was a crisp packet. Someone had been here and littered. Great, just the sort of person I needed stalking around! I picked up the packet and was surprised at its weight; it appeared that something was inside it. Settling back into my sleeping bag, I turned on the camp light. Although the brand was unfamiliar and the pricing was in cents, the crisp packet held a common brown envelope marked 'LUCY X'.

20th April 1975

Dearest Lucy. I hope this letter gets you. I couldn't put it in the regular mail as we are all shot to hell here and the mail is not a priority right now. I have faith in my means of delivery though! This jacket of mine has seen me through some tough times, and it has become a sort of comfort to me, a sort of constant companion.

I don't think I'm going to make our second anniversary, Lucy; things don't look too good and the fighting is getting more intense.

Don't forget to put a pint of oil in the truck every couple of weeks and give old Indie a stroke for me. Tell old Mrs. Robinson to mind her own business when she bitches about the state of our garden. I shall miss our wild garden, and the evenings sitting on the front porch while you get all excited about the moon!

Don't wait for me to return, Lucy.

Live your life and embrace it with all the joy you gave me. Love is not a powerful enough word for how I feel about you.

Bud x

US 60-894-863

It took a while to track Bud's family down, but the internet can be a wonderful thing. I had always planned to visit the U.S., and finding where Lucy lived had been the prompt for my visit. Lucy was lovely, and so were her family. A picture of Bud in the hallway had given me goose bumps; Lucy insisted that I take a copy of it home. I did, and it hangs in my hallway as a reminder of the frailty of life and the wonder of love.

Lucy has the M65 jacket. How it got to me and then to her is a small miracle, but there it is.

There's no such thing as bad weather, just a poor choice of clothing; how true. I'm looking for a new jacket these days. I don't think I will ever find one like Bud's though. A good jacket is a faithful companion when the going gets rough.

Chuck and the Super

Don't judge me. Really, don't. Until you've walked in someone else's shoes, you have no idea what their journey has been like. You have heard this before, right? 'Oh! My life is so bad I had to hit my wife/child/grandmother'. Boohoo!

So, here's a question, but don't answer before you hear my story. Would you kill? Don't worry, I'll ask the question again at the end of my tale. I won't forget; there's not much else to think about on death row, apart from death itself, of course.

An unremarkable life, really. No dramas, just a quiet, grey, dull life, on the outside anyway. At 41, I had gained the girth that my father had died with and lost the hair that he miraculously retained until he was cremated at 72. It was the summer of 1953, small-town USA; I worked in a drive thru joint, loading the occupants of shark finned autos up with Coke floats and burgers and watching them head off for innocent, and probably not so innocent, fun. How I envied them!

Still, I preferred to wait on the customers rather than work in the kitchen. It usually ended in a row with the supervisor, as he threw his weight about barking out ridiculous orders. At least at the service window I would occasionally catch a glimpse of a creamy white thigh before it drove off into the distance.

I returned home to a small apartment with several cats, none of whom were invited, and the contents of two brown paper sacks. One held my dinner, rescued from the joint where I worked, in the other a bottle of Tennessee Whiskey. To say that this was a routine meal would be an understatement. I ate my burger and soggy fries with the same relish that a man with ulcers drinks milk.

You may have guessed from the last piece of information that I live alone. Yes, I do. Fat, forty and financially challenged, not the prize most women lust after.

And then I met Dan.

Dan came into 'The Patty King' the day I worked at the counter. He ordered a vanilla float and a cookie and complimented me on my hair.

He came in regularly after that day, and it wasn't long before I looked forward to his visits. Dan was shy and good looking; when he walked into the restaurant the women immediately stopped their chatter and gazed at him longingly. I guess they may have seen beyond his good looks and seen his gentle easy manner, and wished their own husbands were a bit more like Dan.

You could call me naïve I suppose, but it wasn't until we sat in Lenny's bar drinking whiskey sours and listening to Sinatra that I realised Dan wasn't all he seemed.

It never crossed my mind that Dan was a homosexual; he was an interesting conversationalist and nice fella, and that was a rarity in this small town where baseball is king and real men shoot stuff. It was nice to have someone to share my troubles with; Dan was a great listener and when the supervisor spent most of his day shouting at me and giving me trash can duties, Dan's shoulder was good to cry on.

I can't remember when I fell in love with him, it just happened. Love can be like that I guess; it was all new to me.

And then I met Rita.

Rita strolled into 'The Patty King', asked to speak to Gus the super and ripped into him, telling him what a low-down sonofabitch bully he was and that he didn't deserve good staff like he had. It seemed that she had watched the way he had treated me over time and decided that she was going to act. And boy, did she! Gus sulked back to the kitchen, threw a half-hearted insult at the new help, and stayed pretty quiet for the remainder of the day. Of course, it didn't last, but that day was sweet.

After my shift, she was waiting in one of those electric blue, shark finned autos and we took off to the lake, where she introduced me to what it was like being with a real woman. She was a live wire all right!

My life became quite exciting, I suppose; I was always going somewhere with either of them: the movies, bars, out of town diners, always careful to keep the two apart. Yes, exciting, and wrong maybe, but I was never going back to the loneliness of my existence before I met these two wonderful people.

I could see the fear in their eyes if we were seen together; it was common for us to be harassed by whiskey soaked farmers so we tried to avoid the roadside joints where manliness was measured in shots, both liquid and lead.

Then I fell in love with Rita. I still loved Dan, but it was a different kind of love, and not just the physical aspect. She introduced me to the excitement and joy of life that I had never experienced, but we had to be careful., for different reasons than with Dan though.

Dan stood at the ship's railings, imagining glimpsing through the mist the flaming torch that he had only seen in the newspapers or in grainy newsreels. He was out of cigarettes and the only money he had was stuffed into the lining of his wool jacket. There was a sadness around him that made people avoid his company; most on board had their own problems and were hesitant to hear another's. In the cramped dining area, Dan had sat alone concentrating on his frugal meal, unwilling to meet anybody's eye in case of trouble. There had been plenty of fights on the boat, although now they were nearing New York an excitement permeated the decks and a fresh camaraderie had swept through it.

Irish with Irish, Italian with Italian, and black with black; that was the unspoken rule, and within that a recognised social order. Dan had never bought into this dogma onshore but uncomfortably heeded it now; no need to rock the boat so close to shore. Although there was a new complication; a girl had taken a shine to him and at every opportunity made small talk. Dan had tried to avoid her at first, but Rita's warm personality and entrancing smooth ebony skin attracted him to her. Eventually they sought each other out to share their hopes, dreams and plans for when they reached the new land. He never told her about his sexual preferences, he thought she knew; it never seemed to matter with her anyhow. How easy it was to fall in love! Unexpected but easy. Dan had never felt so accepted, and Rita had never met a man quite like Dan; they found a new courage in each other and, on the last full day before the boat reached New York, they held hands as the waves rocked them against each other.

Unified by a corrupted catholic sense of righteousness, a gang of Italian and Irish took it upon themselves on this final day to right the wrongs of morality upon the bodies of Dan and Rita. They did a thorough job, leaving a black woman and queer man bloody and sobbing on the lower deck; unbeknownst to these thugs, it created a bond and friendship stronger than their thick muscled arms could ever hope to become.

They made their way from the New York harbour together and, with joint resources, headed for California; a long and arduous trip, hitching and riding on freight cars, often sleeping rough, sprawled out in overgrown roadside ditches, out of sight from inquisitive or hostile eyes.

But they made it, and, with Rita's effusive and engaging personality, they soon had work and were able to make a modest home for themselves, albeit carefully situated so as not to offend moralistic types. It would be 20 years until marriage between black and white was legal across the USA, but California had always been more relaxed than some of the other states, so Dan and Rita co-habited without too much intrusion.

Those were happy days. Rita and Dan would return from work and spend the evenings laughing and dancing to jazz records which spun regularly and loud on their newly acquired record player. The boat trip seemed a distant memory now as the California sun eroded painful memories with brightness and heat, allowing Dan and Rita's small garden to erupt in colour and fruitfulness. Food was easy to grow here, and Rita was a good and inventive cook with the produce they grew.

As the years passed, their companionship grew stronger; they encountered some bigotry in the small town, but they were strong in each other, managing to laugh and dance the cruelty of people away in their happy shack.

They both had some needs that couldn't be fulfilled with each other, and soon they were both enjoying satisfying intimacy with those that also had an open mindedness to their way of living. And still their friendship grew; they danced even more in the evenings, as their life together seemed perfect, each one knowing of and sharing stories with the other about the often-comedic situations they found themselves in with new partners. Then they met Chuck.

Rita and I took off in her automobile to places I can barely remember now. They were often spots where the Africans, Puerto Ricans and Mexicans all got their fix of real music and good food. Jazz joints mostly, with ancient pianos and even older players, busting out the blues like the world was ending.

Of course, it was bound to happen one day. I'm not sure if Rita and Dan ever spoke of me before that night, but it sure was a shock to me when on a whim I drove out to one of these joints alone. I was braver now I had seen the world through the eyes of these two wonderful people, and I saw them sitting snuggly in a booth, smoking marijuana cigarettes, and enjoying the bluesman on stage.

It was that night that I heard their individual stories. Stories of man's cruelty to man, and the redemption that their love had brought them.

We were a sorry ménage a trois, but I began to understand that humanity at its best was not as clear cut as it often seemed from the movies and magazines. We continued our relationships separately and together; there was no shame, just loyalty, love and laughter.

It was only an overheard conversation in the diner one afternoon that changed things forever. You see, Gus had never forgotten the day that a black woman had bawled him out. He was too much of a coward to deal with it alone, so one whiskey fuelled night he told his buddies that debts needed repaying.

The plan I overheard was intended to happen that evening. Gus was going to drive his drinking buddies to Dan and Rita's shack and set fire to it, using gasoline that I had seen in jerry cans in the back of his automobile. Hindsight is a wonderful thing; I could have gone to the police. I could have threatened Gus, but this man encapsulated everything Dan and Rita had fought against all their lives; they deserved to be left alone and to enjoy their lives.

I owed them so much. A rage took over me and I formulated my own plan.

It wasn't hard to do. Gus had condemned me to trash duties in the parking lot; his automobile was easy to break into. A few alterations to the battery cables and a shortcut to the jerry cans and it was done.

The death of Gus didn't upset too many people; he wasn't liked and even his drinking buddies didn't attend his funeral. The investigation into his death was brief. But I couldn't hide my guilt, in fact I didn't really want to; I couldn't see myself looking over my shoulder for years to come anyway. I pretty much gave myself up. Dan and Rita were with me every step of the way during my trial. When I was sentenced, they were both inconsolable.

Me? You know, my life was richer for these two and I wasn't sorry for what I did.

So, would you kill? Well, maybe not. I had walked in the shoes of the oppressed for a moment in my life, but I didn't have half the dignity or self-control they showed fellow humans. I killed, and I will be killed.

So, I ask you. What's the difference?

The House

Paul walked past the house of the big guy every day on his way to work. He had been walking past the same house, down the same road, for more years than he could remember. His mother used to say to him, 'Look at that house Pauly, the big guy lives there!' Neither of them knew the big guy, though; they saw people come and go from the house at all hours of the day and night and wondered what the big guy was up to. He never had a name; he was just the 'big guy'.

One evening, as Paul walked home from his work, a man came stumbling down the path from the big guy's house. He was crying and swearing. 'Keep away from that house!', he pointed back, 'you'll get nothing in there but trouble!' and he reeled off into the evening light. Paul took little notice of this, however; the small town was full of nuts, he mused.

Paul worked at a small jeweller's in town; a short walk and bus ride got him there at 8:30 to open the shop and put the displays out. Mr. Rosenburg would come in at 9 and they would drink a coffee and smoke cigarettes before the customers arrived.

Mr. Rosenburg, who owned the shop, was now old, but he still enjoyed pricing the jewellery and making some minor alterations.

One day, Mr. Rosenburg was taken ill. Paul took over while he was in hospital and began to work in the back room, finishing off repairs and getting the invoices sent to customers. On Wednesdays, the shop closed at one and, on this particular Wednesday, the rain fell in sheets, flooding the pavements and hustling the market traders away for mugs of tea and bacon rolls. Numerous watches, rings and earrings were scattered across Mr. Rosenburg's desk; it took Paul the best part of the morning to work out who they belonged to and which had been repaired.

Paul was satisfied with his efforts and thought he was finally done when he noticed a small brown package sitting in a corner. Inside the brown paper was a small gold chalice with unfamiliar lettering engraved on it; it had a small stringed tag with what appeared to be a phone number written on it.

Paul put the bag back in a drawer and decided he would look at it in the morning.

Paul visited Mr. Rosenburg in hospital that afternoon; Paul was shocked at his appearance and thought that Mr. Rosenburg would probably die, which he did that evening, just after Paul left.

'I have no one to leave my business to, Paul', Mr. Rosenburg had said that afternoon through gasping breaths, 'I've made the arrangements; if I don't make it out of here the shop is yours.'

The following day Paul began getting the shop in to some sort of order. Mr. Rosenburg was a hoarder and Paul found receipts dating back to the 1950s tucked away in brown boxes, scattered and secreted all over the back room.

The big guy pondered. And then he pondered some more. People feared him, and he sort of liked that. Some said they loved him, but he didn't really believe them; they were simply scared and thought it would be a great insurance to get on his good side. The big guy knew that people thought he could, well, pull a few strings to get them out of a fix. He did occasionally when it suited him, but it would be nice to meet someone who had no preconceived notion of who he really was, and what he was really like inside.

So, the big guy hung around in his big house while sycophantic people came and went, saying all the things they thought he wanted to hear and bringing him worthless gifts.

The big guy pondered.

Yes, he thought, it would be nice to meet someone plain and forthright.

In the afternoon, Paul rang the number on the tag attached to the gold chalice; a man's voice answered, and Paul explained about the death of Mr. Rosenburg and the gold chalice. 'Oh dear', said the man, 'that's very unfortunate; Mr. Rosenburg was a special friend. Can you deliver the chalice?'

'Er, um', Paul stuttered; the man on the end of the phone said, 'Number 12, Primrose Avenue, thank you ever so much', and put the phone down. Paul put the chalice in his briefcase and made his way home.

Primrose Avenue was part of his route, so he didn't feel too put out. As he counted the houses down, he was surprised to see that number 12 was the big guy's house

As Paul rang the bell, he tried not to think about all the stories he had heard over the years associated with the big guy. A shiver of anticipation ran through him, a feeling that was quite unfamiliar to him. The door swung open and a small rotund figure greeted Paul. 'Can I help you?', he said. Paul explained about the phone call and the chalice. Immediately, the small man, who introduced himself as Mr. Turnaway, became animated.

'Thank you!', he exclaimed, 'do come in! We are having a celebration!' Before Paul knew it, he was led into the dimly lit house. The celebration seemed very subdued, Paul thought; there were many people around, but they made little noise, and where was the big guy? Was the celebration for him? A birthday, perhaps?

Mr. Turnaway took the chalice and placed it on a window ledge; it was then that Paul noticed the unusualness of the windows. They weren't like the ones at home; they were more ornate, some were quite colourful and pretty. Paul was quite anxious to get away from this strange house, but he was intrigued to meet the big guy, so he lingered in the shadows of the large room, hoping that the big guy would make an entrance.

A large man wandered up to Paul and said, 'Do you know him?' Paul assumed the man was referring to the big guy, so he said, 'No, but I've heard a lot about him'.

Then the large man, with a glazed look in his eyes, shouted, 'I know him in here!' and thumped his chest quite vigorously. This unnerved Paul, and he began to seek the way out, but not before stumbling over a tiny old woman, prostrate and mumbling on the floor.

The old woman wailed, and Paul apologised for tripping over her, but she just turned to him with a beatific look in her eyes and said, 'This is how he likes to be addressed', and carried on with her conversation to the carpet.

Paul found his way to the door and was just about to leave when another man, this time oddly dressed in some sort of velvet cape, grabbed Paul's arm and said to him, 'Are you looking for someone?'

Paul, desperate to get away now, stumbled over his words, 'Er…I was hoping to meet the big guy.' The man smiled the biggest smile Paul had ever seen; he thought the man's face might split in two.

The man reached into his cape and pulled out a large book covered in brown cracked leather and, with a mighty 'THWACK!', slapped the cover sending dust mites hurling into the stale air. 'I know him in here!', he exclaimed, 'and you can too!'

Paul opened the door, thanked the man, and hastily walked down the path looking backwards as he went. He closed the gate behind him, noticing a faded sign on it that he had never seen before, '*The Jerusalem Order of the Most Holy*'.

When Paul got home, he collapsed into the armchair with a cup of tea and two biscuits. He felt he deserved them.

Later in the evening, when Paul had calmed himself, he got a phone call from his mother's care home.

'I'm afraid it's bad news', the softly spoken lady on the phone said. 'I'm afraid your mother died this afternoon. We tried to call you, but we could get no answer'.

Paul thought that his mother had died while he was in the big guy's house.

The kind lady on the end of the phone said to Paul, 'Your mother wanted you to know that she doesn't want you to be upset. She said that she was going to be all right now. She said she was going to be with the big guy now.'

Paul replaced the receiver and pondered. He wondered if he should go back to the big guy's house and try to find his mother.

It was all too much for Paul, so he made some hot chocolate and went to bed, hoping things may be clearer in the morning, though he was very doubtful that this would be the case.

Tim and the Whiskery Aunt

Tim was a shy sort of child; he avoided any sort of public appearance, whether this was birthday parties or family gatherings. Unfortunately for Tim, his family were overall quite sociable, and so he often found himself in uncomfortable situations.

He had a whiskery aunt, Sheila, who would press him to her bosom at any given opportunity. Tim shuddered at the memories of the lavender scented woollen jackets that his face was pressed in to when she saw him.

'Oh, Timmy', she screeched, 'how you have grown!'

Tim reddened and squirmed as the ample bosom covered in scratchy cloth was crushed into his youthful skin, leaving him with an aversion to wool and breasts for many years.

Fortunately for Tim, his family lived in a big house with lots of open space where he could escape to if things got too uncomfortable for him.

There was a small wooded glade in the grounds which held all sorts of wonder for Tim. Foxes, birds, rabbits, insects and mice were all his friends; he felt no shyness with them, and many hours were spent with a bottle of ginger beer, a chunk of cheese and bread, and many of the creatures to keep him company. His father regularly berated him for his absence and over sensitivity, but once a social gathering had begun, Tim found it easy to slip away to his woodland sanctuary.

Children, on the whole, are cruel, vile creatures who cut up worms, pin fireworks to cats' tails and burn ants with magnifying glasses. Tim found these dubious pastimes abhorrent, and when he saw the cruelty of his peers engaging in these pursuits he went red in the face, ran home, shut his bedroom door and thought about how he could stop the torment against his friends. Of course, he couldn't; the world carried on turning and the grubby faced urchins persisted with their cruel and bloody games.

It wasn't too long before Tim began to understand that the grownups were no better than the children.

His father often talked of shooting and fishing; Tim spent hours seeking out the numerous traps for mice and mink that his father had set all around the property.

'I can't understand it, Maude', he would splutter to Tim's mother, 'twelve bloody traps with the bait all gone, and not a creature to show for it!'

Tim remained quiet and fearful as his father stomped around the house collecting bits of cheese and wire to make cunning new traps.

One Sunday morning the hunt gathered and his father, garbed in red coat and tails, cheerfully set off on horseback to find old Reynard.

Sunday evening was spent in the living room, with his father regaling the family about the way the hunt had skilfully cornered the witless creature and the way the dogs had torn the red fur to pieces.

'Dear me!', Aunt Sheila exclaimed, spitting crumbs of teacake all around, 'what a terrible shame!'

Tim's ears pricked up at this show of sympathy from his Aunt. 'What a waste of good fur, it would have made a lovely stole!'

And Tim retreated behind his comic strip, as disappointed with his elders as ever.

As the weeks passed, Tim's father attended the regular hunts in the local countryside, and one Sunday afternoon when Aunt Sheila was visiting, (she was always visiting it seemed to Tim), his father presented her with a fox hide. 'There you are!', he proudly announced, 'now you can have that stole you wanted!'

'Wonderful!', she screeched and, admiring herself in the mirror, she held red fur up to her whiskery face with a covetous grin.

It was Tim's birthday, and no matter how much he tried to convince his mother that he didn't want a party she persisted. Tim was dressed in uncomfortable clothes, whereupon several small children, only two of whom Tim actually knew, were brought into the house to enjoy cake and party games. The adults fussed and organised; Aunt Sheila was dressed to the nines and was louder than all the children put together. It was awful. Tim hated the false jollity and commotion the children made, and when a small sullen girl called Jemima threw up her blancmange over Tim's shorts, he decided enough was enough and crept out of the house to the woodland.

As Tim sat brooding under his favourite oak, he became aware of being watched. Looking through the dense gorse in front of him, he could see numerous pairs of eyes looking in his direction.

'What's the matter, Tim?', he heard from behind the gorse bush.

Just as Tim was about to ask who the voice belonged to, several creatures appeared in front of him: Badger, Fox, Rabbit, Mink, Squirrel and Mouse all sat before the perplexed Tim.

The fox inched forward.

'We know it's your birthday Tim, and we have got a surprise for you!'

Tim wondered whether he had drunk too much ginger beer, or eaten something that didn't quite agree with him, but this all seemed very real.

'We have all decided that we would like to come to your party', the fox said. The other animals collectively nodded in agreement. By now Tim was sure that he was dreaming and would prefer to dream in the comfort of his own bed, perhaps with a nice glass of warm milk and honey.

So, he stood up and began the slow weary walk of a boy who must face the questions and jibes of the other children he didn't care for about his absence.

Tim walked up the long set of steps that led to the front door but was aware of being followed. Sure enough, all the animals were following him into his home! Tim thought, 'I must get to bed!'

The party was in full swing; children were playing 'pass the parcel' and the adults were sipping sherry and smoking foul smelling cigarettes. They hadn't even missed him.

Tim walked in with the animals lined up behind him; it took a while before the hubbub died down and the gathering realised that the party had some new guests, of the furry kind. The children cheered, and the adults screamed, but the animals held their ground.

Before Tim's father could take charge, the mouse ran up Aunt Sheila's tweed skirt and the squirrel darted up the tablecloth to retrieve the bountiful supply of nuts Tim's mother had put out for the adults to snack upon.

The children saw a group of cute, furry woodland creatures and thought that this was all part of the party fun; the adults however saw something completely different.

The fox, mink, and rabbit were furless.

They were bloodied and maimed; torn and mutilated flesh hung from their grotesque forms, making their image one of nightmarish horror.

The fox slunk up to Aunt Sheila and sniffed its once attached coat, and the footless rabbit hobbled up to Tim's father to sniff the keyring which held one of its feet as a lucky charm.

The mink had crept into the cloakroom and collected his coat in his razor-sharp teeth and laid it at the feet of Aunt Sheila, who had just recovered from the mouse's expedition inside her underwear.

The only animal which, in the adult's eyes, had retained its fur was Badger. He had another surprise. Sitting on his haunches, he began to pull out clumps of his bristly fur and commenced handing it to Tim's aunt.

'You have used all of us here for your own vanity; perhaps you may use these as a brush to shave your splendid whiskers.'

The children cheered, and the adults wailed, but all the children agreed that Tim's party was the best one they had ever been to.

The Richmonds

The wind battered and bruised the old farmhouse on the hill. Icy fingers reached through every available crack in the old building, forcing its occupant to huddle in the one room that remained habitable during winter.

Rose was pleased that she had put everything away from the outside. Plastic chairs and loose pots tended to end up far away in this sort of weather. She had stored them, along with her new red bike, in the old barn adjacent to the house.

She couldn't wait for the spring; the old house seemed even more lonely in winter, especially since her husband's death last year. The nearby village, albeit small, seemed to come alive in the spring with the influx of city dwellers lodging for a week or two in the numerous cottages around the area.

The only solace Rose had was the TV. Every evening after her chores, she sat down with a small whisky and watched her favourite soap.

'The Richmonds' had been on TV for several years, and Rose felt that she was part of the family. Set in a rural location much like hers, Rose could identify characters in her own small village that matched *'The Richmonds'*.

Rose went around the house, closing doors to keep out the draughts, and checked the locks on the front and back doors before settling down for the evening. The draught and cold that whistled up from the cellar was the worst, and she lay an old blanket across the bottom of the door to help with the insulation.

As she poured her evening tipple, she thought back to the previous year and how she used to pour two whiskies in the evenings. She felt sad that now she couldn't talk to anyone about the most recent episodes of the soap.

Ted had always been as enthusiastic about *'The Richmonds'* as Rose. They used to discuss and guess where the plot was going to lead. After one episode, Ted admitted that he had a thing for *'Briony McKellan'*.

After that evening, they never discussed the show again.

Rose settled herself down in front of the television, pulled a crocheted blanket up over her legs and sipped her whisky.

As the titles rolled and the theme music played, Rose thought about Ted and his comment about *'Briony'*. She had tried to get out of him what it was that he found so attractive about her. Ted mumbled and tried to change the subject, but Rose persisted.

'I like her hair', Ted had replied.

'Don't give me that!', Rose retorted, 'I've seen you looking at those long legs of hers as she gets out of cars! Go on, admit it!'

But Ted wouldn't. And he never would.

After Ted died, Rose had become obsessed with *'Troy Richmond'*. *'Troy'* with that effortless way he had about him, his longish blond hair flopping constantly over his eyes, and oh, those strong, firm legs! But Rose had become angry with *'Troy'*. He started to have an affair with *'Briony'*.

'Briony'! What did everyone see in that tart!

Every evening Rose became more and more angry with *'Troy'*.

'Troy' was now in a full-blown relationship with *'Briony'*, and Rose became apoplectic one evening when the episode showed a long and passionate kiss between them both.

Rose had stopped watching the show after that night and began watching the other channel.

Rose placed her empty glass on the side table and prepared herself for bed. She walked to the kitchen and saw the empty whisky bottle on the table.

'Well. I'll just have to get another!' she said to herself.

Rose unlocked the cellar door, switched the light on and descended the cold stone steps.

The postman was still propped up against the wine cellar, his blond hair flopping out from under his cap, cycle clips around his ankles.

Rose bent down and kissed his cold and now slightly fetid cheek.

'Oh Troy', she whispered in his ear.

Then, standing up and reaching over her husband's body, she took a new bottle of whisky from the rack and made her way back up the stairs.

'I really can't wait for spring to go out on my new bike!', Rose said to herself.

The Second-hand Bicycle

The summer was in its prime; long days and blue skies, the sun blasting its heat on the buildings and roads of Little Puddlebury.

At 15 Royal Mews, James was sweating profusely in his woollen suit and tie. His current customer was complaining to him about the heat, although she was able to wear loose-fitting clothes and then wander out of the shop for a cool lemonade and sit down.

Mr. Cracknell was firm in the matter, 'We run a shop for customers who like old fashioned service Mr. Smith, so a suit and tie you will wear, in *all* the vagaries of the British weather.'

Mr. Cracknell, or *'Rudolph'* as he was known in the staff room, on account of his drinker's nose, was ex-army, so no amount of complaining did any good. Discomfort, he said, was good for morale. The problem was, as James saw it, that he could only afford one suit, and he didn't like to be cold, so he had bought a substantial one. No linen for him in the relentless heat of summer.

'I'm really not sure about this hat', the customer said to him, 'I think it makes my face look…well, round.'

James thought the ugly green hat was a vast improvement on the customer's face but kept the thought to himself. This was at least the tenth hat she had fussed over, and James was having trouble keeping his cool.

'Perhaps I'll try the pink one again', she said.

So, once again, James climbed the wooden ladder in the outfitters shop to replace the green hat, and then move the ladder to get the pink hat. He could feel the sweat running down his legs, and his temper beginning to fray.

'No, I think the blue', she said, just as James had reached for the pink.

James reached for the blue, and felt the ladder begin to topple.

It was exactly at that moment the law of gravity took over; James knew there was not only going to be a horrible clatter as his sweaty body crashed down, he also knew that he would be walking out of the shop door never to return.

As he lay on the floor with the heavy wooden ladder on top of him, he heard a 'Humph!' and saw a pair of brown lady's brogues at his eye level.

'You've crushed that hat!', he heard the woman say, 'I'll go to Franklins instead!' and the shoes disappeared.

James limped home, his trousers torn and the vision of Mr. Cracknell's apoplectic face in his head. James, although bruised and torn, had never felt happier.

He had his wages in his pocket and, after buying several ounces of tobacco and a quarter of Pear drops, was left with a few shillings. As he turned the corner into his road, a black pushbike with rusty handlebars was leaning against a brick wall with a 'For Sale' sign tied to it.

Without any thought, James knocked on the door of the house and gave his last bit of money to a woman who had several children hanging from her. It seemed to James that the money he gave her wouldn't go very far, but she was delighted and offered him a glass of milk as he 'looked so worn and beaten'.

James sat at her kitchen table with the glass and was soon surrounded by children of varying ages, who had varying levels of mucus running from their noses. 'Where you goin' mister?', one of the bolder children asked. 'Oh', said James, 'I'm off on a long bike journey around the countryside.'

This was news to the child, but more astounding to James, as the idea had only just popped into his head. It sounded a splendid idea though. The woman looked at James with, what it seemed to him anyway, a longing that she would like to accompany him.

'Well, I must be going', James said. 'Thank you for the milk, it was most welcome.'

'That's fine, dearie', she said, 'I hope you have a good holiday, it's lovely weather for a bike ride.'

'Won't you take this as well?' she said, handing him a small knapsack. 'I'm sure I won't need it as much as you.'

James was touched by the frazzled woman's generosity; underneath her tired and worn exterior he thought he could see a pretty young woman with a life of adventure in front of her.

'I have a sister about 20 miles from here, she lives in Wensbury. If you go there, be sure to call on her and say hello from Janet. That's me. Her name is Bernadette. I'm sure she can give you some refreshment if you pass.'

'Er, thank you', said James, hoisting the knapsack onto his shoulders.

After some careful manoeuvring around small children, he walked down the path to collect his new bicycle.

As he cycled down the road towards his small house the smell of blossom filled his senses, increasing his appetite for his new adventure. This enthusiasm was quickly dampened by the sight of his fiancée standing outside his house, arms crossed, with a face that spelled trouble.

'About time you showed up, you were supposed to meet me at the park, and where did you get that thing…...

'don'tthinkI'mgoingtobeseenwithyouonthat…!'

James sat on his new bicycle looking at his fiancée's lips moving and imagined that he was at the fair, and he had to shoot ping pong balls into her mouth before it closed.

It would be easy, he mused. As the clatter of words fell from her lips, James realised that his bicycle could whisk him away back to the sound of birdsong and tumbling streams.

She must have read the look on his face.

'If you go now', the lips carried on moving, 'you won't ever see me again!'

James realised in a split second that this was not an altogether bad thing.

His legs engaged with the pedals, and before he had a chance to reconsider, his new steed took him off down the lane with the sound of his fiancée's voice decreasing with every revolution of the wheels.

James 'whooshed' down hills, panted up others, then sat by gurgling brooks, refreshing his feet in the cool waters. A farmer's daughter sat next to him that first day away from the town. She had strawberry blonde hair and a freckled nose.

They sat on the banks of a brook watching the sticklebacks weave between their toes. She brought him sweet fresh milk and bread, and after eating, took him to a secluded woodland glade where the formalities of his life were erased in twisting limbs and gasps of pleasure.

With no awkwardness, he left the girl, as they brushed leaf litter off each other's nakedness, laughing at their messiness.

The daylight hours were spent exploring the lanes, and evenings finding company in small inns, where he was normally befriended by kindly souls who satisfied his hunger with ale and home cooked food.

Often, he would meet cheery faced girls, who took no heed of town ways, and took as much ale and cider as he, belching and laughing at their own rudeness. Then he would lay with them, head spinning with too much cider, but sober enough to appreciate the magnificence of the moment.

A twisting perfume-laden lane led him past a painted and carved wooden sign reading 'Wensbury'. The name seemed familiar to him, but he couldn't recall why.

Stopping at a long rose clad wall which surrounded a big house, he rested his back on its warm bricks and ate the last of the pie that had been given to him in the previous village.

Drifting into a comfortable sleep, he was rudely awoken by giggling and girlish chatter.

Opening his eyes fully, he could see that the girls had woven daisy chains and wrapped his slumbering head in them; his bicycle had received similar attention as it stood, leaning on a tree before him.

As James stood, smiling at the game that had been played on him, all but one of the girls ran off. She was a dark-haired thing, reminiscent of his fiancée, but without the sharp edges. She wore a country style white smock, which hid a comely figure.

'You may be the lad on the bike then', she said. James smiled at the supposition.

'That I be', he replied, trying to hide his amusement from her.

'And you are?' he said.

But no reply came from the sweet lips, just a coy smile and a flounce as she turned and walked away down the winding lane.

'Well', James pondered to himself, 'whatever next!', and, mounting his bedecked chrome steed, cycled leisurely in the direction she was heading.

The news of a man on a bike had preceded him, and as he entered the village proper, old men and their wives peered from open windows and doors as he cycled past, nodding greetings at them as he went.

Toothless hags smiled, and young housewives laughed as the daisy bedecked bike went past them. The girl from the brick wall was among them, standing with an older lady, she with several small children tugging at her petticoats.

'Mary told us what she done to you, poor lad!', the older lady said.

'Come in for some tea and cake, while I feed the young un's. I'm Bernadette, and you are?'

'James', he replied.

Bernadette led him into a small kitchen filled with copper pans and the aroma of freshly baked bread.

Sitting at the table, she poured a cup of tea for him and placed a giant slab of fruit cake in front of him while Mary sat opposite, gazing at him with dark pooled eyes.

They sat for hours it seemed to James. Bernadette fed the children from the pantry as they came; gammon ham, bread, cheese and, for the youngest, a milky white breast was given, removed from her floral dress without the absurd need for modesty in this cosy home filled with laughter.

It seemed natural that James would be given a bed to stay in, and that his stay would run into days, and then weeks, as he began to help out on the land, earning his keep. The bed was no more than a hayloft, but the most comfortable bed James had known, especially when Mary crept in with him at the end of the long hot summer days. His life had never been better.

Working on the farm one day, James received a blow to the head as a stone flew from the plough. He felt fine but went back to the hayloft to rest for the remainder of the day.

Waking from a restful sleep, he was surprised to find he was laying on a cold hard floor. Opening his eyes, he saw concerned faces peering down at him.

And one irate one.

'Well Mr. Smith, that was a stupid thing to do. I'm glad you're awake now; I think you'd better go home for the rest of the day.'

The voice of Mr. Cracknell jolted James as he lay prone on the floor. Lifted to his feet, James looked around and to his disappointment found the old shop was just as he had remembered it all that time ago.

Squinting, James staggered out into the sunlight and began the weary walk back to his home. He thought about the vision of the small kitchen of Bernadette, and the happy sound of her children playing. But even more he thought about Mary's soft and willing body, as they lay together in the hayloft on those long summer nights.

As he turned a corner into his road, a pushbike lay against a brick wall. It had rusty handlebars, and dead, withered daisy chains were wrapped around its frame.

James walked on.

He must get cleaned up before meeting his fiancée this evening.

A Million Housewives

Richard and Crump had been friends forever. Of course, Crump isn't a real name; it was shortened from *'Crumpet'*. No-one can really remember why; whether it was in honour of the hot buttery delicacy or the fact that he 'couldn't get any', the naming was lost in the mists of sherbet lemons, tobacco smoke and ale.

Needless to say, the nickname had stuck and even though Graham had grown and got a steady job, every time he got back with the boys the cheer went up, 'CRUMP!', and he was transported back 40 years to the school playground where he had first received the title. And he loved it.

Richard drew the tobacco smoke from his roll up deep into his lungs, as he watched Crump puff and pant up the steep Derbyshire hill. It had become a sort of annual adventure for both, although the adventure side had diminished over the years, as worn knees and sore backs had led them to shorter walks and discussions on ailments rather than women.

They were both moderately unfit, but the Derbyshire air always lifted their spirits, and they usually returned to London with healthier complexions than when they left, prompting resolutions of gym memberships and jogging, which were always unfulfilled.

It was the last day out on the hills and Richard was looking forward to getting home to a hot bath, and his even hotter wife.

It amazed him that he had managed to find such a woman who he not only still found attractive after 20 odd years, but who also made him laugh and feel good about himself. Even more amazing to him was that she seemed to feel the same.

He had some suspicions over the years that she had seen other men, but he was too afraid of confronting these suspicions and had filed and hidden the thoughts away from his less confident and juvenile self.

Crump would have been shocked if he had known about Richard's self-doubt. Over the years, Richard had professed to have an encyclopaedic knowledge of the 'female sex' and their ways.

After marrying Linda, Richard had become the envy of his boyhood gang. It was as if he had won all the school trophies in one fell swoop, and then married the unreachable stunning head girl. He wondered if they envied or pitied him, ('punching above his weight there, I reckon!') and felt sure when he returned from the toilets in bars that conversations quickly changed.

Crump came to a stop next to Richard and slapped him on the back. 'I wonder how many more years we'll be able to do this', he said through wheezy gasps. Richard looked at his old friend and thought the same.

He also wondered how long he could stomach Crump's jolliness and constant positivity. It wasn't as though he had much going for him, a small flat and an even smaller salary. Crump had the knack of being a natural socialite, although he had never married, and seemed to find female relationships hard to sustain.

They had stopped in a small village a couple of hours previously, the well-stocked poky shop smelt of mothballs and damp, the proprietor looked as though he smelt the same.

Brown shopkeepers' jacket, with a once white shirt, egg stained tie and flat cap finished the stereotypical picture of northern-ness.

A few years before, they had stopped in the same shop, and Richard could remember the dour face and smell as if it were yesterday.

They picked up a few overpriced items for their last evening's meal under the stars; sausages, eggs, and a tin of beans. Richard smiled to himself as he looked at the tin, remembering Linda's endearing rendition of the old TV advert for Heinz beans. After many years together the childish humour never failed to amuse them both, as she flirtatiously sang the advert for him.

'All set for a feast tonight, then?', Crump exclaimed with his characteristic jollity. 'I can't wait to hear you farting all night after those beans!'

Richard smiled, and inwardly groaned at the thought of Crump's snoring, leaching through the night air between tents. At least he was not sharing a tent as in previous years; the smell created between them after beer and beans was noxious, to say the least.

They had been on these expeditions for more years than he could remember; it seemed churlish to stop them now, but Richard felt that maybe they had run their course. Richard became more irritated every year with Crump's minor habits; the noisy eating, constant commentary as they walked and, worst of all, the night terrors.

Crump seemed to have suffered with these all his life, although he denied them, and awoke irritatingly cheerful; he was surprised when Richard emerged from his tent in the morning, bleary eyed from another night's disturbed sleep.

Crump loosened the shoulder straps on his rucksack and rested it against a boulder while he went off to satisfy nature.

Richard sat with his back on the rock and finished his cigarette.

A flash and buzz erupted from the side net pocket of Crump's rucksack, as his mobile phone received a message. Richard glanced at the pocket which held the phone and was surprised to see the sender's name LINDA disappear from the screen.

'Ah, that's better!', Crump emerged from a small clump of rocks zipping up his trousers. 'Shall we push on, then?'

Richard nodded and hoisted his own rucksack onto his shoulders, striding along the path as he did so. As the light began to fade, they looked for a sheltered place to pitch their tents.

'I don't understand why you've never settled down, Crump', Richard blurted out as they both hammered pegs into the rocky ground, 'I mean, it's not as though you are ugly or anything!'

'Why, thanks for the affirmation, Dick!', Crump retorted. 'Guess I haven't been as lucky as you are finding a pearl amongst the swine.'

'You think Linda is attractive then?', Richard mumbled, as he grappled with a guy rope.

'Are you kidding! She's bloody gorgeous!', Crump bellowed through the increasing wind. He laughed to himself at the ridiculousness of the question.

As the light decreased and camp was set, the primus stoves were lit for the last time. Richard brought out from his tent the few remaining items that they could cook for dinner.

As usual, the ingredients for the meal were eclectic, due to all the decent stuff being consumed on previous nights under the influence of real ale and subsequent single malt whiskies.

'So, let's have a stocktake', Crump announced exuberantly.

'Let's see, two rashers of bacon, one dubious vegan sausage, six slices of bread, three squashed tomatoes, one packet of instant mash, one pork pie, and a can of baked beans. Well, not exactly a feast, and God knows what we will have for breakfast, but let's get cooking, Dick!'

As Richard began to use the can opener on the baked beans, Crump looked at him and began singing in a corny way… '*A million housewives every day, pick up a tin of beans and say...BEANZ, MEANZ, HEINZ!*'

Something clicked in Richard's head. A text from Linda, and Crump's obvious attraction to her; it all made sense now. The reason Crump hadn't mentioned any relationships was because he was having one with his wife!

'Remember that advert, Dick?', Crump said.

'Why wouldn't I remember it' Richard snapped back, 'Linda sings it all the time. Why would you suddenly remember it!'.

'Well, why shouldn't I, it was part of our growing up!'.

Richard stopped the slow revolution of the can opener. 'I bet you have a real good laugh about this, don't you, Crump!'.

'What are you saying, Richard?'.

'I'm saying you have a real good laugh with my 'gorgeous' wife while you're shagging her!'.

'You're crazy!', Crump replied…but any further discussion was interrupted as the tin of beans, already half open, its jagged edge covered in orange sauce, flew through the night, hitting Crump squarely on the forehead.

'Fu………'

Crump slumped back, bringing the awning of his small tent comically down over his face.

Richard sat and looked at the tableau before him; a bean splattered half collapsed tent, with a pair of legs sticking out the front.

'Crump?'

Richard got up and pulled the sticky nylon fabric of the tent away from his friend's face. A tent peg, one of the batches especially bought for the trip, ('Will break through the toughest ground campers!'), stuck out of his friends' neck, the green luminous top glowing resolutely in the dimness ('You won't trip over them in the dark either!').

'Crump?'

Richard looked closer at the tent peg. Knowing Crump, it had probably only been half-heartedly hammered into the rocky ground and been the perfect angle for his unfortunate neck as he toppled, driving it messily through his carotid artery. Richard wondered whether 'A terrific method of killing!' could be added to the tent pegs' advertising campaign.

A brief illumination lit Crump's deflated tent.

The phone.

Richard reached past his friends' lifeless body and pulled his rucksack out into the open. He fumbled with the mesh pockets and retrieved Crump's mobile. He clicked on 'messages' and found the one received earlier from Linda.

'Hi Crump, I hope you are both having a good time! I hope you are keeping an eye on R for me after I confided in you! He's been incredibly stressed lately, so make him laugh! Is he doing ok? Don't forget the song when you have baked beans, it makes him chuckle every time! Thanks, old friend...We both love you! PS. I have a friend who is interested in romance, I have told her all about you!!! X'

Richard stood and looked down at the prone figure on the ground.

'I wonder', he thought, as he walked towards the barely visible cliff edge, 'how did they know it was a "million housewives"?'

It seemed an awful lot to him. If he hadn't got other plans, he might have done some research on that figure.

'A "million housewives"? Impossible' he thought, as his foot stepped over the rock face and out into the void.

The Coffee Shop

Dave settled into his favourite seat in the coffee shop he visited once a week. It was his treat, almost a guilty secret.

He sat near the door so that he could glance out of the window and see what was going on in the small market town.

It was market day today, but there didn't seem to be a lot of people around. Perhaps it was the grey drizzly weather putting people off from going outdoors?

Dave always brought a book to read, and he took his new book, bought last year from a charity shop where he got most of his reading matter from, out of his shoulder bag and placed it on the table top.

The waitress walked over and, smiling, placed his black coffee in front of him. As she retreated, the air was tinged with the perfume that she always wore, but now it was mixed with the aroma of the food and coffee that permeated the shop and her clothing.

The coffee was deep brown and had a caramel froth in the centre.

It had been served in a rainbow striped mug; a request Dave always made, as he disliked the fussy cups the shop normally offered which he could never quite hold comfortably.

He wasn't quite on first name terms with the waitresses, but he felt that he was a regular now. The routine, up until recently, had been steady; same table, same coffee. He'd had a conversation with one of the waitresses; she had been trying to stop smoking and Dave had shown sympathy in the process. He had some experience with the same issue some years ago.

Unfortunately, in recent weeks, he had slipped back into the habit.

There were few customers in the shop. The usual older ladies out for gossip and a couple of middle-aged men in business suits. The two older ladies, who seemed to time their visits with Dave's, appeared subdued today. The bird-like chatter that usually accompanied their meeting had been replaced with nervous glances around the shop and whispered exchanges.

The waitresses themselves were all dressed in black, which was the uniform of sorts; they seemed less ebullient than usual.

Their dark dress code added to the more sombre tone that seemed to permeate the shop and there was no light-hearted banter between them.

Dave loved to 'people watch' and see the way the waitresses were with each other and then with the customers.

There had been times previously when a difficult customer had prompted hidden (or so they believed) conversations between the waitresses behind the counter. No words could be made out but the glances and body language between them allowed Dave to make his own version of the dialogue.

It was a quirky type of place. The first part selling food and drinks, incorporating the seating area that Dave used.

Towards the rear of the shop was the stock of organic produce; tins of fruit, bags of porridge, coffee, tea and numerous foodstuffs that Dave had never even heard of. Bottles of cider and beer from local breweries were also on offer. Clothes, jewellery and novelty items made up the remaining space in the shop.

It was rare that Dave wandered down towards all of this; he was usually happy just to sit, watch people and, when this became tiresome, read his book.

Reading was the best part of Dave's visit.

He'd almost forgotten how satisfying it was to crack the spine of a fresh book and sip his coffee whilst immersing himself in a new tale. There was something pleasing about being unsocial in a social setting. For some reason, the hubbub of the shop's business rarely stopped him from enjoying his reading time.

The two businessmen had finished their drinks and went to leave. The larger of the two apologised as he squeezed past an arriving customer. The new customer, a young mother with her toddler, muttered something under her breath to the man while giving him a dirty look. She moved quickly out of his way with her head down and stood in front of the counter to order.

'Bloody people', she uttered to no one as she stood, purse and child in hand, at the counter.

'Clean your hands with these', she said to the child, passing her a packet of wet wipes.

Wearily, the waitress smiled and took the fractious woman's order. The woman glanced nervously around the shop looking for a seat for them both. Her eyes briefly met Dave's while she scanned the shop.

She quickly looked away and, after paying, walked with her child to a far table where she used another wet wipe to clean its surface.

Dave lifted the mug to his lips, savouring the fresh coffee smell and the reassuring weight of the mug. It seemed that a full mug left him at least 30 minutes of reading time. He opened the new second-hand book and began to read.

His taste in books was eclectic, but among his favourites were sci-fi and horror. There was joy in a new read, sometimes great disappointment too. He had learned over the years that it was okay to ditch a book after a chapter or so. There was only so much time left in life, so you needed to fill it with good stuff, not the dross!

The toddler began to whine as the mother scrubbed the child's face with yet another wipe. Dave could tune out most things around him when engaged in a book, but a child's whining or crying left him irritated.

Adjusting himself in the chair, he began to read. Then, quietly and without fuss, he closed the book and, standing up, left the shop, leaving the book on the table alongside his full cup of coffee.

The waitress puzzled at Dave's quick departure, walked slowly over to his table and began to clear it. She would keep the book for him when he came back in.

She opened the book to the first page……

'Early in the twenty first century, a terrible virus swept across the planet, killing two thirds of its population….'

Printed in Great Britain
by Amazon

50239588R00113